Sex

Meds, Reincarnation,
Livin' The Covid

Life

Sex

Meds, Reincarnation, Livin' The Covid

Life

By Eric Robespierre

ISBN: 978-1-7365781-1-7
LCCN: 2021924263

Published by Eric Robespierre
www.ericrobespierre.com

Also by Eric Robespierre

The Yummy Hunter's Guide
The Best-Tasting, Low-Calorie Foods and Where to Shop for Them
(With Helen Brand)

Cracking the Walnut
How Being a Little Nuts Helped Me to Beat Prostate Cancer

Living Large in America
The Life and Times of the Family Ginsburg (pronounced Du Pont)

Lighten Up and Log In For Love
How Humor Helps Baby Boomers Survive Online Dating

We Gave Them Life, Now They're Trying To Take Ours
How To Successfully Communicate
With Adult Children Before It's Too Late

Sex, Meds, Livin' The Covid Life

ACKNOWLEDGEMENTS

S ex, Meds, Reincarnation is the sequel to Sex, Meds, Livin' The Covid Life. As with the first book, I owe the same debt of gratitude to Robert Leung, my former agency art director, who again showed his brilliance when I asked him to create a second cover. To Angela and Audrey for their diligent and superlative copyediting. To the multi-talented, Richellb, who again designed the book's interior and cover of my book and formatted the e-book.

To my friends and family whose love and support continue to get me through the dark times.

"Each night, when I go to sleep, I die.
And the next morning, when I wake up, I am reborn."
—Mahatma Gandhi

FOREWORD

I began writing *Sex, Meds, Livin' The Covid Life* to escape the virus by going into a world where I could find sexual pleasure beyond my wildest dreams. I was lucky because, being a writer, I usually live a good part of my life in the world of fantasy, so the move was easy peasy lemon squeezy. My timing was also impeccable. I finished the book when the promise of a Covid vaccine was on the horizon. What's the line? Man plans, God laughs.

Another escape was in order, so here comes *Sex, Meds, Reincarnation, Livin' The Covid Life*. In the first book, the characters are so dazed and confused by the threat of the virus, that Bernie, my protag-onist, attracts women because they think they will be having sex with a famous movie star. What woman wouldn't want to sleep with the second coming of Don Juan or Shakespeare?

You do not have to read the first book to enjoy this one, so thank you for your interest. I hope it does for you what it did for me and allows you to escape these very scary and uncertain times.

THOMAS WOLF
WAS WRONG

It takes a real man to be reincarnated as a woman. Otherwise, to learn you're Mary F'in Shelley don't you know you'd be Fucked-NineWaysToASundayInTheCemetary?

HeyHeyHoHo, there I go again, jumping ahead of myself. Slow-TheFuckDownThereChampo! Let's start from ScratchARoony!

I was already in an ExtraVirginOliveOilFragileStateOfNormalFuckedUp when the invite hit my inbox because, my FellowSapioSuckerSapians, just one hour ago, I discovered Meryl stole all my Hanky-Pankies and cleaned me out of MEMEANDME!

I don't mean to make excuses. Had I not been on the verge of taking my own life, I'd have remembered the Thomas Wolf book, *You Can't Go Home Again*, and never have listened to Gerry when he told me ReincarnationWasTheRoadToThePus-Say.

"It's two o'clock in the freakin' afternoon Boyo, and you're still in your skivvies!" He brought his face closer to the screen. "And, what's with the smile? You injectin' Botox into your cheeks, or you just happy to see me?"

Fuck me; why am I on FaceTime with this asshole?

"Meryl's gone," I muttered.

He didn't know whether to shit or get off the pot, and I took delight in his inability to come up with a putdown, or was it he had so many and couldn't make up his mind which StingMeSillyWillyZinger he'd zap me with.

"Well, look at it this way, Boyo..."

He swiveled his face into a LincolnPennyProfile, striking the pose until I had to laugh, as he knew I would, despite having seen it ManyManyMuchoMuchoTimes since he first pulled it in the second grade.

I couldn't contain my smile until he ruined it with another dig.

"Got tired of your side of the street, did she—the old rug muncha?"

No point in bringing up the fact that the old rug muncha was twenty years my junior, and had a workout regime the envy of women half her age. Enjoyed sex like it was being recalled the next day; and looked to give me the sweet afterglow as much, if not more, than any straight woman I'd ever encountered.

"I say you're better off, Laddie Boy. All the little Vs you been gulpin' like candy to keep up with your LuluLemonLady may make your dick hard, but it fucks with your BP, cuts the O2 to the ole brain, and that's why you can't think straight Boyo."

I had nothing for him, so I continued staring at the screen.

He gave me one of his WhatTheFuckIsReallyFuckin'YouUp looks and finally said, "You don't have the Covid, do you, Boyo?"

I picked up my non-contact infrared thermometer, shot myself in the forehead for probably the fiftieth time today, and said, "Look— 97.9!"

"OkayOkayOkay! Take a f'in shower, get dressed, cause I know how to chase away your blues, get you back on the PelotonExpress-WayToHeaven—ReadyTeddyToLickAndSuckTheNewPus-Say!"

He saw I didn't react, so he pushed his face right up to the screen. "Don't make me call your upstairs BabyCake; tell her to check her floor cause Mr. Peepers from 10E drilled a f'in hole in his ceilin', so he can watch her brush her brush in the mornin'."

This is what I have to deal with!

14

Let me also tell you... besides Meryl stealing half my identity, that the only way to get SomeSome was reincarnation, and as a f'in woman, yet, there was another sharper stick in the eyeball reminding me of that infamous day. Get this one, my FineFeatheryFriends! *Reincarnation* can also make you *immune to the Covid*!

I know inquiring minds want to know. But of course, I searched my closets twice more, looked under my bed, in the kitchen closet, even emptied my laundry hamper, but no Hanky-Pankies. Meryl even got The Hank Moody leather braided bracelet in black and brown made by Flongo; she had to have carefully snipped it off because it was so tight on my wrist. Otherwise, I'd have felt it and awoken from my sleep.

To save me from the Covid, I became a Dirty Boy, and to succeed as a Dirty Boy, I went from being Bernie Max to David Duchovny to The Hanky-Panky Man to finally morphing into a KickAssFour-Way. Still, when Meryl stole my Hanky-Pankies, naturally, I thought Covid would get me, so how can you blame me for what happened next?

After Gerry read me the riot act, I decided to make a good impression, so I put on a nice clean white shirt. Unfortunately, I hadn't worn it in over a year, and it was irritating my neck, and I had the urge to rip it off and play with my nipples, but I held back and smiled, and out it came, TheLamoDribbleDribble. "Okay, Gerry. I'm all ears," Drip—drip—drip.

"Boyo, I want you to open up your email and look for the message from BackAgain.com," he commanded as soon as we got back on the coms.

"BackAgain.com?"

"That's CorrectoColonFullStopInTheNameOfLove, BackAgain. com."

I mussed up my hair and gave out my best maniacal grin. "Here's Johnny!"

"Nicholson—*The Shinning*—that's good. Obvious, but good." He smiled.

"Oh—come on! You know I do a good Jack!"

"OkayOkayOkayCutTheComedyBoyo, I get it. The f'in wheels came off your LoveMobile because the bitch Meryl ran you through The-FuckYouOverBlender, and you got TheItchyTwitchyFeelin'Boohoos, so Laddie Boy, like always, I'm gonna save your FraidyCatPussy-WussySnowFlakeRentBoyAss."

I threw him my FaceTimeFistBumpFuckYeahAirSalute, to which he replied in kind.

"So Laddie Boy, since the pandemic hit, there's been a shit load of new website copying our site, trying to lure the Dirty Boys and Girls away with all sorts of giveaways, and shit, so Dr. Keys..."

"Dr. Keys? Who's Dr. Keys?"

"Dr. Keys is da man, Laddie Boy! Da man who created the Dirty Boys and Girls Hookup site. Dr. Keys wrote The Code!"

"Ah, that Dr. Keys!"

"And like all geniuses, Dr. Keys understood being first takes you only so far. Once he created a site for the Dirty Boys and Girls, he instinctively knew somebody would copy it and eventually figure out a way to lure customers away, so as soon as he launched the site, he began thinkin' of the next big thin'."

"Ah, forward-thinking by going backward?"

Gerry held the stare just long enough that IKnewThatHeK-newThatIKnewSockItToMeWasComing. "Sarcasm does not exist in this dojo, does it?"

"No sensei!" I shouted.

We both laughed, and I had to hand it to Gerry, who knew fuckin' with our favorite lines from *The Karate Kid* permanently lowered my level of anxiety.

"You know Bernie, forget I asked you to open your email, read the invitation and pull up the site. But in your FuckedUpStateOf-Mind, I'm gonna save us the half-life of plutonium and show you on my iPad."

Now, who was being sarcastic? But shit, I wasn't going to say anything because he was right. I was in a FuckedUpStateOfMind.

I leaned forward, waiting for my lesson.

"Alright then! So what we have here is the Home Page that gives you the pitch."

Then he read, *"I am certain that I have been here as I am now a thousand times before, and I hope to return a thousand times. – Goethe"*

"Classy, right. Like this, Goethe was a big fuckin' deal. Am I right, or am I right? Like you're the brainiac, right Boyo?"

"Yes, Goethe was the real deal and considered the greatest German literary figure of the modern era."

Gerry beamed.

"But, I never remember anything about him being interested in reincarnation," I added.

"Live and learn, Laddie Boy—live and learn."

He winked, then scrolled down the page and continued reading. *"The soul is not born; it does not die; it was not produced from any one… Unborn, eternal, it is not slain, though the body is slain. – Katha Upanishad"*

I threw up my hands. "Before you ask, I have no clue who that is."

"Not to worry, Laddie Boy. He's there to set up the UndercoverAgent."

"The UndercoverAgent?"

"When you want your site to hide its true purpose, so only members know the real deal, you set up a cover. That way, the Providers won't know you're doing anything illegal."

"The Providers?"

"The companies that house your website. Match-Making sites are one thing, but hookup sites for sex are a NoNoNanette. That's why Dr. Keys came up with The Code."

I nodded. I got it. "SomeSomeQuickyLickySuckySecretSecret-SomebodySpecialSpecial."

He grinned. "But like I said, the doc knew there'd eventually be competition...SoWhatToDoWhatToDo?"

"Reincarnation? "

"Tell me, how much more desirable were you when the babes thought they were suckin' Duchovny's cock, or havin' his lips lick their clit?"

"Hey, I didn't..."

"YeahYeahYeah, you might not have promoted it, but you f'in took advantage of it, aye Laddie Boy? "

I had nothing.

"HeyHeyHey, tell it like it is! We all want to be special, and we get special by being rich—pretty—famous, or we fuck or marry someone special. You followin' me, Boyo?"

"Yes," I said, recognizing TheTruthAsGerryKnowsToBeTrue.

"Listen up then. There's one more thing that makes us special."

"And that is?"

"If you're related to someone special. If mommy's a movie star, daddy's a rocker, and if big brother's landed on the moon, guess what—you're GetSomeSomeAnytimeYouWantSomeSome!"

He raised his hand. We gave each other a FaceTimeFistBump-FuckYeahAirSalute.

Gerry beamed enough energy to light up a Times Square Billboard. "You got it now, huh—Boyo?"

"Gerry, you think if I'm related to say—oh, hell, I don't know..."

"Casanova!"

Shit, I had to suffer even more facial electricity from Smilin'Gerry-TheSmartAss.

"You'd name him, wouldn't you? You f'in Pussyhound!"

"Yeah, I named him. Wouldn't you think Casanova gets more pus-say than—say—Bernie Max?"

"As far as I know, I don't look like him, and for that matter, neither do you, Gerry."

"And how the fuck do you know that, Boyo?"

"I've seen the movie, and *we* don't look like Heath Ledger."

Gerry puffed out his profile.

"Maybe Bob Hope." I laughed.

"He was good enough to get Joan Fontaine! BingoBoyoBingo!" It was his turn to laugh.

I gave him that, but the question remained, so I asked, "So, Gerry, how do I—*we*—get to star in *Casanova's Big Night?*"

As soon as the question left my lips, I felt my rectal muscles tighten, and I knew this was the opening Gerry was waiting for. Like any good boxer who knew this was the end for his opponent, he hit me with the one-two combo: TheShowAndTellYouYouDumbFuckSmirk immediately followed by The ShowAndTellYouYouDumbFuckSermon.

"Ever hear of somethin' called *Facial Recognition*, Laddie Boy?"

There was something in the way he pronounced Facial Recognition that set my neurons firing through my cerebrum and bursting across my synaptic motorways in a pyrotechnic display, the equal of any Macy's Fourth of July finale.

I pulled my white-tee off the back of my chair where I left it instead of putting it away and neatin' up the place before my Face-Timing, and wrapped it around my head turban style, and held up a piece of white paper to my forehead.

"The question, hermetically sealed in a mayonnaise jar on the front porch of Funk & Wagnalls since this morning, is... 'Who can make me so famous, women will fuck me silly?' The answer," I paused, "Dr. Keys."

Gerry genuflected. "All hail Carnac The Magnificent!"

We broke out in laughter at one of our most famous Johnny Carson routines, skits we used to repeat the morning after we saw them.

Finally getting a grip, Gerry pointed to the Homepage. "Screw matchin' birth dates, astrological signs, and GraveRobbin'DNA. *Facial recognition*, Laddie Boy! And, not just any facial recognition, but what Doc Keys has developed is light years ahead anythin' on the market. I'm talkin' StrangersInAStrangeLandFacialRecognition!"

I couldn't help but catch the wave. It was the HallelujahHallelujah HealingMomentWhenYouGotUpFromThatFuckin'WheelchairAndWalkedForTheFirstTimeInYourF'inLifeHallelujahHallelujahHallelujah!

OkayOkayOkay, I wasn't under any revival tent, and Gerry hadn't completely turned into Elmer Gantry, but as I said, I caught the wave. I could have jumped to my feet and sang "Fever." Unfortunately, I hadn't returned as Peggy Lee, so I simply let the wave wash over me and waited until Gerry delivered the closer.

"As far as the world knows, Facial Recognition software involves identifying, or verifying someone's identity by using characteristics and features of their face. You know that, right, Bernie?"

Of course, I would have known that had I given the subject a second thought and done my due diligence, so I nodded my agreement quickly in the hope Gerry would get the message and promptly end his lecture.

This was not to be the case, and he continued.

"Then you also know they use 3-D vascular heat-pattern and skin texture analysis, but mostly algorithms to identify certain points on the face, like the shape of the chin or lips, to create a template. Then when you get your face scanned, it goes into a database, and it's compared to the templates in that database. Right. Right?"

"Yeah—sure. But Gerry, I'm impressed. Where did you learn all this technical stuff? Vascular and what was it, heat—something and skin—something?"

"Vascular heat pattern and skin textures. You think I was goin' to get into this without doin' a little research?"

"So, Gerry, when I see someone in a movie put their eyeball up to a screen, some program checks to see if they're already in a database, and if they are, they're allowed to pass through a door?"

"Live retina scanning. Yeah, that's the ole fashioned way. What I'm talkin' about is matchin' you up by just usin' a picture of your face."

"You don't have to be in the room..."

"Only need your headshot."

I thought about the implications, and then it hit me, and I got it.

"You—I mean the person you match up with—they don't have to be alive, do they?"

"BingoBangoBoyo, and that's what makes this guy such a freakin' genius!"

"But I thought they use your retina because it's unique only to you? How can they get the same result with a photograph?"

"Ah, that's the magic of his software. It breaks the pixels apart into its DNA and matches chin to chin, lips to lips, and most importantly da ole schnozzola because..."

We both said it together, "the nose knows!"

"Indeed it does, Boyo! That's because the nose, aka, the olfactory system to those in the know, get it—those in the *know*—is connected by nerves and shit to the brain's limbic system. Guess what the limbic system controls, Boyo?"

He laughed, and I gave him an IDon'tKnowHowMuchMoreOfThisShitICanTakeEyeRoll, provoking another rumble of laughter.

He smiled triumphantly and announced it as if heralding in the name of his newborn. "Memory, Laddie Boy—fuckin' memory! Everythins' stored in those memory cells, and I mean everythin' since the beginnin' of time—cause nothin' is lost in your DNA; nothin's forgotten." He took a breath. "DNA—that's all your shit. All the fuckers that were you—made you into the fucker you are now! Capiche?"

21

The dots were coming together. Could this be true? Is it conceivable that my DNA—the DNA from my ancestors—all reside together in my brain as one happy bunch of memory cells? Is it possible that information could be retrieved, brought up into my consciousness, and become actionable?

Gerry was looking at me and thinking pus-say. I was looking at him and thinking, could my ancestor's DNA make me immune from Covid?

TRADECRAFT AT
TRADER JOE'S

I'm still figuring out the best way to double mask. I have one N95, two black cloth masks, a box of KN95's and two boxes of surgical masks. I got the N95 as part of a survival kit the city gave out during Sandy. I wore it once, but it was uncomfortable, plus I didn't want to fuck it up in case of a real emergency. I'm partial to the cloth masks that I can wash right after using.

I decide on one cloth and one surgical, but in what order? I experiment and choose surgical on the inside and fabric on the outside. Two reasons. It looks better, and more importantly, I can breathe better.

I don't walk more than two minutes before I realize how uncomfortable this arrangement is, so I remove the cloth mask and decide to double up when I get inside Trader Joe's. I figure the paths in Stuyvesant Town aren't that crowded, and when they are, I'll just duck out of the way or choose another route.

At 14th Street and Avenue A, I see both sides of the avenue, the crowds around the entrances to the L line. I can easily skirt them and the bus stop where people are waiting for the M14. There is no sidewalk line at Trader Joe's, so I have no problem entering, and when I take the escalator down to the main level, the place isn't crowded, so I'm thinking, maybe I don't have to double mask.

I know my way around, so I start at the cheese display and work over to the Vidalia onions, along the way picking up hummus and blueberries. On the other side of the fruit display, I hear someone sneeze. *NoApplesForMeMotherFucker!*

On with the second mask, MyFineFeatheryFriends! Okay-OkayOkay, I don't need to be Euclid to know it would be a stretch for the viral particles to float up into the air and carry over the fruit display and then DropDemDeathDroplets onto my mask. Still, the father of geometry doesn't have to take the risk, does he?

I stop in my tracks. Wouldn't it be a pisser if Euclid were in my gene pool, swimming to me from the Fourteenth Century? How ironic if he'd come now, instead of when I nearly flunked geometry. You know, I still have the occasional nightmares about being trapped in an equilateral triangle—ThankYouMuchMotherfucker.

I pick up cereal, crackers, orange marmalade, bananas, get onto the back of the line, knowing I can grab milk, yogurt, and orange juice along the way. I don't see anyone sneezing, but that doesn't mean the unidentifiable offender isn't among the group, or he could be coming up behind me. Shit, I don't even know if it was a man or a woman, but the semi-autonomous, convulsive expulsion of air from the lungs through the nose and mouth is SoScaryFuckingLoud, I'm assuming male in origin.

The line is moving, and everyone's sticking to the rules and hitting their circles, so they stay the required six feet from the closest shopper. I'm looking over to the flower display thinking I'll jump off, but heads are into cell phones, so I can't chance to lose my place. When I get to the cashier, I'll run back and grab the pink Dahlias and yellow Chrysanthemums. StrangeThingsAreHappening! I never was into flowers until the pandemic, then, WhatHoBernie, I get up the nerve to go back to Trader Joe's, see the flowers, and wham-bam-thank-you-ma'am, I'm bringing home enough bunches to fill up my living room and bedroom vases. Vases that belonged to my dad and were gathering dust on a top shelf of a kitchen cabinet.

The milk and the juice weigh the most, so the cashier separates each; nevertheless, the two bags are heavy. Once I get about a hundred yards into StuyTown, there are plenty of benches, so I sit, go, sit and go until I make it home. Do I worry I'll catch the Covid from sitting on a bench? The thought crosses my mind, but I'm outside, and from what the medical experts say, the virus doesn't stick to surfaces. Experts also say chances are slim you will become infected when you're outdoors unless someone less than six feet away sneezes directly into your face.

Yeah, well—FuckMeNineWaysToASundayInTheCemetary—I'll just take those two pieces of advice, plus anything else that comes along regarding Covid with—TheyDon'tFuckingKnowWhatThey-Don'tFuckingKnow! Translated means: if you get a QueazyUneasy-Feeling, go directly home without stopping, take a hot shower and then relax, BernieBabyBubbie.

"Laddie Boy, why the fuck don't you have your stuff delivered? That's what Amazon lives for, as does FreshFuckin'Direct, or one of the other food delivery apps. Shit, haven't you been usin 'em?"

"Instacart. I've been using Instacart."

"So why the fuck did you stop? Right to the door, right?" I nodded, and Gerry smiled.

After showering and putting on fresh clothes, I had FaceTimed him because he was anxious to know if what he told me about Dr. Key's revolutionary new idea had got me ReadyTeddy to get me SomeSome on BackAgain.com.

"Lemme see the flowers. You're not going down Gay Street, are you, Boyo?"

I walked over to the vase on my living room windowsill, brought the arrangement back to my computer.

"Pink? What the fuck! Show me your fuckin' wrist!"

Before I could react, he was doubling over in laughter. "I'm just fuckin' with you, Boyo! The BabyCakes love you got flowers. Makes 'em go all soft and MushyWhooshy, thinkin' you're Prince-Fuckin'Charming, kinda guy bring 'em romance, not just the Fuckie-Suckie. Nice fuckin' touch, Laddie Boy. You just may well turn into the ManlyGoldenStud, Laddie Boy—YesIndeedeeYouJustFuckin'May."

JACOPO SANNAZARO

G oddamnMyEyesAndGoodByeToTheHankyPankyMan!Iwould be more than BubblyBubbly to learn I was the reincarnation of this 16th Century Italian poet, humanist, and epigrammist from Naples.

HeyHeyHoHo, look at me now, Mamma! I wrote in Latin and created Arcadia, f'in Arcadia, that glorious idyllic land anyone who was anyone in European literature copied. Come on up, get into my conscious brain, LemmeLemmeHaveHisStuff!

I kept my excitement in check as I listened to Gerry raise his to a fever pitch. Sannazaro, TheFuckerFromNaples, as Gerry called him, was catnip to the women of the court of Frederick IV who swooned over Jacopo's poetry; still my pal was going for bigger fish, and that fish was Casanova.

"Look, Boyo, don't get me wrong, I don't mind workin' for the pus-say."

He began singing.

"I'm happy readin' poetry
Take my time
I'll see you when my love grows
Baby, don't let it slide
I'm a workingman in my prime
Readin' poetry"

I had to admit, Gerry could capture a tune. "Van's the man! Am I right, or am I right?"

"You are right!"

We did our FaceTimeFistBumpFuckYeahAirSalute.

"But I'm da hound, not da poet, ya know what I mean, Jelly Bean?"

"But Gerry, you're doing okay, right? I mean, otherwise, maybe..."

"Don't you get PussyWussySelf on me, Laddie Boy. This site is golden!"

He threw me a tiny grimace. I tossed back a nod signifying how seriously I took his reprimand and would never again question the site's legitimacy.

"I'm the last to admit it," he giggles. "But I don't handle disappointment too well, and as I told ya yesterday, I was thinkin' Casanova, or at least be the guy who wrote the Decameron. Man, that was one great PussyTale, Laddie Boy."

"Giovanni Boccaccio," I said

"You knew that off the top of your fuckin' head?"

"Actually, I was looking up your guy, and he led me to Boccaccio."

For a brief second, I thought about lying, but I wasn't that low on TheSelfEsteemLadder yet.

"So, you do know what I'm talkin' about?"

"Did you know your guy Sannazaro influenced Boccaccio, who influenced Casanova," I said?

"Six degrees of f'in separation, is that what you're sayin', Laddie Boy?"

"I do believe Senor Sannazaro wrote his share of poetry that unlocked many a bedroom window and a maiden's chastity belt." I winked. "Where do you think they got the expression—the pen is mightier than the sword?"

"OkayOkayOkay, I get your point. You made your tib, Boyo."

"Touché!" I laughed at his one-upmanship.

"So, Dr. Keys used my photo from the other site?" I asked.

"Yeah, scanned the shit out of it."

"And from that photo, the good doctor can decipher my past lives?" I shook my head. "That's f'in unreal!"

Gerry looked down at a pad lying next to his computer. "Damn, I wrote it down...neuronal stem cells, neurogenesis...fuck, I can't read the rest of it..."

For some unexplainable reason, I turned and saw my reflection in the mirror across the room. Could this face hold the key to my past? Could women want to fuck me because they think fucking me was like fucking someone famous?

I stood and stared at my computer screen.

FuckedNineWaysToASundayInTheCemetary! What the hell did Gerry get me into this time?

I MUST HAVE SLEPT FUNNY

I'm standing in the empty vestibule of a doctor's office separated from the crowded waiting room by a glass partition. The doctor, who I don't recognize, materializes out of nowhere. The first thing I notice and admire is her shelf-like ass that I begin to caress. She doesn't complain. The doctor is from the Middle East with a sallow complexion, deep-set brown yearning eyes whispering a terrible sadness. I find her erotic and cannot believe she appears to desire me. She stands on tiptoes and kisses me full-on. Her kiss is warm and luscious. I'm embarrassed, afraid someone in the waiting room will see me, in particular my father. JUMP CUT. I'm ready to defend my actions when my father, who acts as if he hadn't seen the embrace, hands me a set of car keys, and in Italian, tells me we have to go to his villa in Fiesole. I take the keys. JUMP CUT. I'm in the street, and a man is lying dead on the sidewalk. The Rolling Stones approach, wearing plague masks and dressed in medieval costumes. Nobody cares about the dead guy. JUMP CUT. I'm in a Sea World-like amphitheater watching Mick Jagger stare into the pool. There is something ominous in the water. It's black and snake-like larger than any reptile I can picture. Mick, wearing a red Speedo, nods to the audience and dives in. JUMP CUT. Mick's leaping out of the water in the embrace of a dark-skinned beauty half his age, yelling, "I love my antibodies!" JUMP CUT. I'm sitting in the compartment of a 19th Century train, explaining to Gustav Mahler how much his 'Resurrection Symphony' means to me. Gustav's more interested in the line of naked women on white horses riding along-

side the train, waving black flags. JUMP CUT. I'm getting out of my father's 2000 red Cadillac Eldorado, and he's yelling, "Leave the doctor, and take the keys!"

ABOUT LAST NIGHT

"Look, I'm the last person you want to tell—not because I don't love ya—because you know I do—and you know I won't judge ya—you know I won't—and you know I'd help ya—you know I would—but Bernie—I don't wanna know what a sick fuck you are."

I felt myself going numb and felt dizzy in the head and knew if I got up, I'd fall.

He began to giggle. "Man, when you lose your laugh, you lose your footin'." He made the sound of a cuckoo bird.

I felt the blood rush to my face.

He just stared at me, waiting.

Oh, you fucker, I know that quote!

"He who marches out of step hears another drum!" I yelled triumphantly, throwing back another of our favorite Cuckoo's Nest lines."

"BingoBangoBoyo! Just playin' with ya!"

We threw each other FuckYeahFaceTimeFistBumpAirSalutes.

"Boyo, you wanna know what I think about your dreams?"

I nodded.

In that split second, I realized, maybe Gerry, this crazed Pussyhound, could provide insight; otherwise, why would I tell him about my dreams?

"It's obvious; you got someone from your past tryin' to talk to you."

It can't be my dead father because he couldn't speak Italian. Then again, how could I have understood him? Is it possible I speak the language? I visualized my disembodied head sitting on a pike atop a merry-go-round horsey when Gerry suddenly banged on the table, and I WokeTheFuckUp!

"It's your Reincarnate, Boyo! That's what the fuck's happenin'!"

What kind of sick fuck sees his disembodied noggin sitting on a merry-go-round horsey? Not to worry, my FineFeatheryFriends, I am a quick study and a testament to how a sick brain can multi-task so without missing a beat, I brilliantly replied, "You think that's what's happening, Gerry?"

"Indeed I do, Laddie Boy, indeed I do. Tell me more Memory-DreamShit. Don't be a ShyPussyWussy. Free your PsychoSelf, Laddie Boy, free your PsychoSelf!"

Actually, images were coming back into my head as he was talking.

I closed my eyes. "I'm in an Italian Palazzo, and I'm attending a wedding. Everyone looks like they're from a da Vinci painting."

I tightened my lids until they hurt. "Mr. Miyagi, dressed as an Italian Prince, approaches and says, "Whatever you do, don't change your name.""

"Fuck! You're a woman, Boyo!"

I opened my eyes, closed them again. "Then—then—I'm in this enormous room; huge chandeliers, fancy furniture, red drapes. Waiters dressed up like—you know those Renaissance troubadours, come through the curtains. They are holding large trays of flaming meats high above their heads. Suddenly, the heat from the flames sets off the sprinkler systems, and we're all drenched in water! I mean, we're all soaked to the skin, and I'm being pulled out of the room by Mr. Miyagi, but he's dripping wet and looks like shit."

I opened my eyes and began laughing. "FlambéedFloodedAndFuckedUp!"

I HEAR YOU KNOCKING...

You know you're going down the rabbit hole when you yearn for the days you heard voices. WhatToDoWhatToDo? YouGotIt-YouGotIt! I dug up my Hanky-Panky Amazon receipts, thinking reordering would prompt HIS return.

HE would reassure me once I wore my Hanky-Pankies, that I'd be MyselfHisSelfOurselves again and wouldn't be afraid of StrangersInTheNight entering *Our* SubconsciousHideawayAndPrivateDreamstateLivingQuarters and taking over our conscious behavior.

Let's face it. It was EasyPeasyLemonSqueezy, after the Hanky-Panky Man went bye, bye, for you fuckers from out of the past, you 14th Century Italian Reincarnates (probably carrying the f'in plague), to get into our brainpan. Then use our Amazon passcode to purchase medieval costumes that'll make me look like an escapee from Dante's Inferno!

But this is all SoNotToWorryLaddieBoy, BecauseBecauseBecause, according to Gerry, TheManrootWantsWhatTheManrootWants and if that means pretending you're the DNADrip out of a 14th Century vagina so you can make the Johnson happy, just fuckin' do it!

Let's face it; aren't we already doing fuck-all to make the Johnson HappyHappierHappiest? Isn't Magical Viagra already juicing up my Willy Boy and transforming him into the BoyWonder? So, I ask you, my FineFeatheryFriends, why not go for a jolt of the good ole DNA?

I WAS PUTTY IN HER PALM

Her name was Madame Evangeline, and her fame had reached down to my boyhood pal Barry in Boca West. Who knew he was interested in this palm reading shit? AnyWhoBooHooBooHoo, when he came up for a visit, that's what he wanted to do, and I said, WhatTheWhoBooHooBooHoo and agreed to meet him at Chez Max on a Sunday morning, where Madame Evangeline did her thing. (OkayOkayOkay, so maybe I was ItsyBitsyTeenieWeenieYellowPolkaDotBikini influenced by the fact my last name is Max.)

I live on Twentieth and Ave C, so to get up to Sixty-First and Third, the quickest way is the M23 cross-town to the 6 Train to Fifty-Seventh and Lex. The trip should take an hour, but I always give myself an extra fifteen. So when I reached the subway entrance and learned from pissed-off passengers streaming up the stairs there wasn't any uptown service due to police activity, I sprinted to the corner, just in time to grab the M1 that would take me up to Madison and Sixtieth.

Now, I am talking BackInTheDayNobodyGotMeACellPhone; when you either had to successfully deal with your GonnaBeLateAndGetScreamedAtBeauseIDon'tCareAboutThePersonI'mMeeting, OrOrOr, give yourself heart palpitations, chest pains, hives, whatever the fuck you do to self-destruct and mess up your body when life gets in the way, and you cannot control the uncontrollable. You feel me?

Many a Sunday morning, I took the M1 from 23rd and Park Avenue South to 60th and Madison and then walked west for two blocks for a weekend outing in Central Park. The trip takes about twenty minutes because traffic is always light and not many people board before 57th Street. That said, after missing the train, my sense of reality went out the window. Instead of trusting the normalcy of the bus route, I called upon my coping mechanism, i.e., TheBullshitI-TellMyNervousSelfToKeepNervousMyselfFromLosingMyLunch, that if things got hairy, I could always jump off at the next stop and grab a cab.

I white-knuckled it, several times nearly bolting for the exit but deciding as the bus sped past one stop after another to stay put. I stopped sweating around 57th, so by the time I got off and then walked the two blocks to the restaurant, I was pretty confident I no longer smelled like a dog in heat.

Trust me. I had no idea Madame Evangeline was anything more than a charlatan, or worse—so misguided, she believed in her Palm-ReaderBullshitBunkum. If Barry chose to believe in this PRBB, go to it. I would get my jollies by reminiscing over a delicious omelet, those ultra-thin frites, and a couple of glasses of Beaujolais Nouveau that always tasted better in a French bistro.

"We observe the principles of reincarnation everywhere in life: the cycles of nature, day and night, the cyclic motion of the sun, earth, moon, and solar system. We also see the principles of reincarnation reflected around us each day: a plant grows, dies, and releases its seeds. Its seeds burrow into the earth, begin to sprout, and new life is reborn once again."

How could she see that in my sweaty palm? Well, with two glasses of Beaujolais—HellBellsChristmasTimeCameEarly so when my eyes met hers—the SynapticPathwaysOfLustAndDesireOpened and MyMadWomanOfTheEvangeline could have recited the Fuller Brush Manual, and I'd have swallowed it, hook, line, and SinkerMe-DownBoyI'mFallingFast.

"Reincarnation, or the rebirth of energy, or life, occurs all around us in different shapes and forms every day. Perhaps this is why to many of us reincarnation is something intuitive, something that resonates the very nature, the very essence of life."

And that was all she read, folks. So, after two more cups of coffee, and thanks to the carafe of water and extra croissant, I was confident my stomach lining had adequately absorbed the vino. And I wouldn't feel dizzy or nauseous when I went to the bathroom; a trip that would carry me past the table where Madame Evangeline was sitting and having her Espresso break, and the perfect time for MeSeniorSmoothMove to make his play.

IKnowIKnowYouKnowIknow, you would think after such a thought-provoking reading, I'd have a thousand questions that needed answers, but in reality, there was only one question requiring a reply—was the Manroot going to get what the Manroot wanted?

Madame Evangeline was flipping through an issue of Architectural Digest when I paused, caught her eye, and proceeded to give her my best pick-up line, this side of 'Are you good with a whip?'

"My friend Barry," I said, pointing over to Barry, "is one heck of a photographer, always shooting homes and interiors for AD, so maybe he could do a photo of you that you could post at the door..." —wait for it here comes —"but you already knew that you just read his palm."

Madame Evangeline didn't bother looking over to Barry and when she smiled I knew she wasn't buying any of my bullshit.

She took my hands in hers and said, "We see that our lives, and everything around us, follow a fundamental pattern; that of change, growth, transformation, and evolution. We see that all of life goes through a maturing process at different rates and different velocities. Thus to many of us, the maturation process of the soul, through the process of reincarnation, sounds as instinctively and fundamentally correct as other maturing processes in life."

FYI, my FineFeatheryFriends, processing information like the heavy shit she just laid on me starts with input from the sensory organs that, in my case, were awash with Beaujolais Nouveau. Madame Evangeline knew once the vino cleared my system her words would soon register in my cerebral cortex, and I would understand 'thoughts are things...thoughts are things'.

A SHOT IN THE ARM

"Can you believe this shit, Laddie Boy?"
We were FaceTiming while at the same time watching CNN.

"De Blasio looks like a train just hit 'em."

"Allison's hitting 'em hard over closing indoor dining, and I think his answers are pretty weak."

"I'm glad I don't own a f'in restaurant; those poor bastards are really gettin' the shit kicked outta 'em."

I noticed he was all duded up, and it was only eleven o'clock.

"You have a hot date?"

"Right on, Laddie Boy; right the fuck on!"

"From the website?"

"Roger that! Remember Gina Lollobrigida, Laddie Boy?"

"Who doesn't?"

"*Trapeze* that was my favorite, and guess what, Laddie Boy?"

"No telling."

"Tina's a pilates instructor and former gymnast."

"Tina's the reincarnation of Gina Lollobrigida? I didn't even know she died?"

"She didn't, Laddie Boy! Tina's the reincarnation of Piera Borsani. She just looks like Gina."

I had two cups of coffee and a cream-filled doughnut—actually two. One I ate on the way home, and the other I'd finished seconds before connecting with Gerry. It was that SugarySweetiePie that electrified my NeuralBullshitNetwork and made me say, "Piera Borsani—the poet who lived around the time of Dante—how cool is that!"

Gerry laughed. "Fuck it, Bernie, how do you know all this stuff?"

I gave him the shrug. You know, the shrug that says, 'Ah shucks, it's nothin' really'.

Then he gave me a look that says, OhYouHadMeGoingYouFuckButYouAreSoFullOfShitYourEyesAreBrown...that look.

"Okay, who was she?" I said finally as my last sugary neuron crashed and burned.

"Star of the '28 Olympics! Was the f'in Michael Jordan of Women's basketball! Plus—listen to this—listen to this—she won gold at the '28 Summer Olympics in the discus throw. She was a freakin' animal, a freakin' animal!"

"Where's the meat,' I giggled.

"So, what's that supposed to mean?" He snarled.

"Animals are meat eaters, right?"

"You sayin' I can't handle her because I don't have the meat? You're not attacking me—TheManWithTheManlyGoldenManroot, are you Bernie?"

Oh, SynapticShitStormshit! "NoNoNo...you are the man, Gerry! You're the MeatEatingManWithTheManlyGoldenManroot!"

Gerry, not sure whether to buy my excuse or come through the screen and punch me, chose the former. Fire no longer leaped from his eyes when he calmly said, "She's a vegetarian. She takes excellent care of her body."

I gave him my best IBetterKeepMyMouthShutOrElseI'llJustFuckMySelfEvenMoreSmile.

"Okay, Laddie Boy, I'm gonna let this attack on my ManlyGoldenManroot pass because I know you're massively FuckedAndConflicted by Mary Shelley messin' with your testosterone levels."

41

"Conflicted? What? You think because I'm the reincarnation of a woman, I'm light in the loafers?"

"Whoa, Nelly! You might like *Beaches* a little too much, but I never thought you were gay as a picnic basket, Laddie Boy". He laughed. "But enough about me, let's talk about you. What do you think of me?"

It suddenly hit me. "You dick! That's from *Beaches*! You saw *Beaches*?"

"Had to, Laddie Boy, had to. Remember, Susan Garfield, that gorgeous redhead from Queens Village? Only way I was gettin' SomeSome was to see the flick. AndAndAnd, *Sweet November* was another GoAlongToGetSomeSome."

He looked at me and smiled, "Worryin' about losin' keeps you winnin'." Then he blew me a kiss.

"*Sweet November*—that's from *Sweet November*! And you—you told me *Goodfellas!* No wonder I could never find it! Fuck you, Gerry, and the horse you came in on!"

"GottsTaKeepUpWidDaQuotes, Laddie Boy!"

I composed myself, loaded up a notable quote, and gave him both barrels. "You know Gerry; Lord Krishna tells us whatever you are attracted to at the time of death, you'll be born as in your next life." I smiled. "Better watch out Gerry, you'll come back as a muscle-bound discus thrower."

THE KEYS TO
THE KINGDOM

I did a Jacques Cousteau into the literature and discovered changing sex is not all that unusual when examining a person's past lives. Some researchers had gone so far as to indicate that reincarnation bolsters the idea that gender is neither male nor female but a spectrum that runs the gamut—a variety, so to speak. This information calmed me down and took away my AngryBoyFace. Consequently, when Dr. Keys came up on the screen and introduced himself, my body was totally relaxed and the smile on my face genuine.

Thank goodness I gave myself some extra time because I messed up the first connection royally, but when the clock struck three, I fixed the problem and saw the prompt informing me the doctor would be connecting with me momentarily.

I was surprised by his youthfulness and the fact he wore a yarmulke and had a lithograph of *A Night at Saint Evangeline-de-Luz* by Man Ray prominently displayed on the wall behind him. Now, there was an image that looked as if it magically played with perspective, giving you the feeling you were traveling down that street. For a moment, I experienced SameTimeTravel; only I wasn't going forward. I was going back into my previous lives.

Oh, this Keys, he definitely likes to fuck with your mind!

"Mr. Max, a pleasure to meet you. I hope you were able to set up the link without too much difficulty?"

"No—no problem." I looked past him to the Man Ray. "I like your artwork," I said.

He smiled, not with his lips and mouth that he kept motionless, but with his twinkling eyes and a raised left eyebrow. I had a philosophy professor who could do that. I later heard he was sleeping with his female students and therefore associated that expression to be one of I'mNotHearingYouJustThinkingOfHowYouMadeMeComeLast-Night.

"Thank you," he said. "I always enjoy meeting fans of Man Ray and the school of Dada and Surrealist movements."

I had nothing for him and hoped he wouldn't question me further. I'm one of those who know a little about a lot, but not a lot about anything.

He put on huge, black, horned-rimmed glasses changing his expression from I'mNotHearingYouJustThinkingOfHowYouMade-MeComeLastNight to I'mAPrayingMantisAndCanMindFuckYaFella-SoWatchYourPsAndQs.

"Bernie—may I call you Bernie?"

Sure, Just don't call me late for dinner! NoNoAndNo, I held the MoronChildInMe in check and simply nodded.

"As I wrote to you in my email, I like to select a new member randomly, so I can gain a bit of insight into why they chose our site, how they are experiencing it and what they hope to accomplish."

He removed his eyeglasses, and his expression changed from I'm APrayingMantisAndCanMindFuckYaFellaSoWatchYourPsAndQs to one that asked, "How'mIDriving?"

"But first, Bernie, I'd like to know more about you."

I heard myself say, "I have always believed life and everything around us follow a path."

He smiled.

Oh shit, it's Him!

He continued, "A path of change, of evolution—reincarnation."

He smiled. I smiled, or was it The Voice making me smile because sure as hell; he was the fucker talking, not me.

"So, naturally, when I heard about BackAgain.com, I assumed it was a..."

Keys waited and fuck me; I had nothing.

"Band of brothers!"

Goddamn, The Voice was throwing a no-hitter!

I looked up at the litho, and suddenly I felt myself inside the picture, traveling down the street in Saint Evangeline-de-Luz, and I wasn't alone. The Hanky-Panky Man was by my side, and together, we were going all the way.

After the connection ended, I'm pretty much shot and hit the bed. Hearing The Voice, no—having the Voice take over and control me was a shock to my system. Nothing negative. No nausea, dizziness, or the warning signs of a heart attack, but my pulse was racing, and I knew I had to calm myself down. I took a couple of deep breaths and began to meditate.

I heard Keys' voice as I meditated. He was asking how I was dealing with the pandemic? Had I been tested? Was I interested in participating in a COVID-19 vaccine clinical trial?

My iPhone beeped. For a moment, I had no idea where I was. I looked over, and it was Gerry FaceTiming me. I sat up, grabbed the Lemon Lime Gatorade from the nightstand, took a swig, and opened the connection.

I cleared my throat. "Howdy!"

"So, how'd it go with Keys this morning? You said you'd call afterward. What's up?"

"Did you know he was Jewish? Wore a yarmulke? And, he was a kid? He couldn't have been more than thirty-five. Shit—I was wearing socks older than him."

"No kiddin'? I coulda sworn he's older than dirt, all the degrees and shit listed up on the site."

I decided not to mention A Night at Saint Evangeline-de-Luz, or my trip down the painted street, or my sudden realization of the connection between that and a certain palm reader of the same first name.

"He was very impressed when I quoted Lord Krishna."

"Of course he was, Boyo."

"I didn't want to embarrass you, that's all."

He smiled; nodded.

"Gerry, I have to tell you, he acted more like a therapist. The way he asked questions. He freaked me out."

"What do you mean, Boyo?"

"He kept asking about my health?"

"You didn't tell him about fuckin' David Duchovny, did you, Laddie Boy? You didn't screw the pooch for us, did ya?"

"Not my mental health, my *physical health!*"

"Okay, don't get your drawers in an uproar. You mean the Covid? He asked if you had it?"

"He lives here in Stuyvesant Town."

"He lives in your nab! No shit!"

"Coincidence—I think not!"

"Roger that, Boyo. Roger that!"

"I think because he's a shrink, management contacted him, asked him to provide counseling."

"He give you any numbers—tell you if anyone in your freakin' buildin' got the 19?"

"He told me not to worry."

"He said that? Not to worry? Those were his exact words?"

"And he knew about my prostate cancer. He said that wouldn't be considered an underlying problem."

"Holy shit! How the fuck did he know about that?"

"You won't believe this, but he bought my book, has it in his waiting room. He said he recommends it for anyone with prostate cancer or any cancer. He said that employing fantasy to help one get through a crisis is a proven psychological technique."

We both yelled it together, "Another coincidence—I think not!"

"He also said something about how fortunate I was to have excellent genetic traits that would provide further protection."

"I knew it! I fuckin' knew it!" Gerry was up, yelling, "FuckYeah-FaceTimeFistBumpAirSalute!"

I leaped up, joined him.

"You're golden, Laddie Boy—golden! Well—fuck me! It's because of Mary Shelley—MaryFuckin'Shelley! I looked the bitch up in Wikipedia. She's one f'in big deal—husband, too!"

I sat back down. "Percy Bysshe Shelley. Major poet, I know."

"What kinda a name is Bysshe? Frutti tutti if you ask me."

"Old English. Landed gentry, artisto, probably common then."

He smiled. "Did you know she fucked around? Got herself preggers with Shelley's kid when he was already married."

"No, I didn't," I said. *I had no idea where Gerry was going with this.*

"Shelley's first wife committed suicide. And you were the cause of it."

I was getting tired of the third-degree and the put-downs but hadn't the PsychoPseudoIntellectualCohonalEnergy to form a resistance.

"You come from some real dirtbags, Boyo!"

That cut it. The riding had to stop. "Gerry, what the fuck!"

"Just playin' wid you, Boyo. Really jealous MaryTheMerryHarlot, got a whole f'in page when my guy got UngotzungoolBupkis-NoneNadaZip."

He gave me the thumbs up. "That CalifornicationLookAlike-Stuff is just shit compared to what you got swimmin' in your StudsAndStarsReincarnationGenePool, Laddie Boy. You are a real hell-raiser, Boyo! The women are gonna be comin' for you."

"I'mReadyTeddyGoManGoToLickDaPus-SayAndGetThe-SuckyLucky!"

It was The Voice. Holy shit! Bernie Max never talked like this?

THE FAUTEUIL
AND THE BERGÈRE

B efore I go right into my first French Furniture Dream, I would like to provide some context. The Hall of Mirrors is in the Palace of Versailles, and Lydecker Hunt is one of New York's most prestigious interior designers. I am working in an antique shop called Île-de-France. The owner, Evangeline Morris (Madame Evangeline when she's reading palms and how I refer to her), and Lydecker Hunt both went to Clemson, and to Lydecker's credit, he's always looked after Madame Evangeline and made sure to take her on at least one of his European buying trips.

Why it's me and not Madame Evangeline in the Château can be simply explained this way—it's my f'in dream! So, let's get it on.

I'm in the Hall of Mirrors, and I have to drain the snake. Now, Lydecker Hunt of The Hunts Of Columbia, S.C. is HighFuckin'Falutin. Peeing is below his station in life so, when a guard ceremoniously lifts a red velvet rope to allow MrPretentiousPants to get up-close and personal with The Fauteuil a la Reine, I shove a hankie into my pants and hope to hell, it sops up the TrickleWickle. JUMP CUT. I'm in Île-de-France, and Rod Steward is testing out a fauteuil. He's dressed in black leathers with his shirt open at the neck so the world can see every religious symbol known to man hanging from enough gold and silver, that when melted down, could feed an army for a year. When Rod inquires about the chair's provenance, and I say I have to ask the owner, he says to make one up. I cannot believe someone so obviously religious could ask me to lie. JUMP CUT. It's my first day alone in the shop when MissSnootyTootyHautyCouture exits her chauffeur-driven limo and enters the shop. She immediately informs me she owns an island (judging by her reedy-thin appearance, it's obvious it's barren of anything edible). She then corners me against a late 18th Century French oak marriage armoire and demands to know if age and provenance determine whether a Fauteuil or Bergère is the more valuable. Having just learned a commode is not a toilet I'm full of myself, so when I see she's wearing white cotton gloves, I figure I'll get her going by either sneezing or slipping her a Xanax. JUMP CUT. I'm alone in the shop, and I'm looking at the pair of white cotton gloves the woman has left on an 18th Century Guéridon *side table when the chair begins to speak to me in French.*

I recall waking up and saying to myself, what the fuck! Then I started to search my RemembranceOfTalkingFrenchFurniturePast. Sure, the woman with the white gloves had come into the shop and mentioned she owned an Island, but as far as the rest of the dream, that was total bullshit.

ButButButBut I could smell the smoke coming out of my ears from my inhibitory neurotransmitters blocking the transmission of the YouAreNotFuckingGonnaBelieveThisTalkingFrenchFurnitureSignal to my WhatTheFuckIsTheMatterWithYouBernieDendrite.

NowNowNow, thanks to the dream, it was all coming back to me. Madame Evangeline had gone off to visit another dealer, leaving me alone in the shop. I'm in the back away from the windows and any distracting street traffic taking photos for our website when I hear the male voice (small v), as opposed to the BigGuyVoiceVersion1.0, from my Hanky-Panky days.

At first, I thought I was just talking to myself. You know—you ask yourself a question in your head, and you get an answer—*(that voice)* right away.

I looked up that type of behavior on the Internet (where else) to see if I was crazy and discovered it's all RickyTicky. FYI, when you speak out loud, the muscles in your larynx move and activate the left inferior frontal gyrus, also known as Broca's area. NewsBreak-NewsBreak—same f'in thing happens when you SilentSpeakToYourDumbAssSelf.

AllCoolHandLuke until the voice, small v, speaks to you in French and not off the dinner menu at ChezTooFuckin'Expensive-ForMeMonAmi. Anyway, to get back to TalkingFrenchFurniture, thanks to owning a DVD of Les Misérables, I got the gist of it.

First off, he wants to make it absolutely SophiaLightCandleStyle-TiereChandelierWithCrystalAccentsClear that only a BlueBlood-Buttski was good enough to sit on his CushyCushyAubussonTapestry-CoveredCushions. He then went on to proudly name each count and countess and the festive occasion of their SitDownski!

Naturellement, he was none too pleased when one sit-tay was a FattyFatAsski that had to twist and turn, shift and squirm, wiggle and writhe to get ComfyComfy. AndAndAnd—*Mon Dieu*—what about when the FatAsski had to get up and out? Just the thought of him repeating these painful maneuvers without destroying MonsieurFussyFauteuil was almost as terrifying AsAsAs—when a servant sneaked a SitDownski during their cleaning rounds. Ever hear a Fauteuil squeal? Trust me; you don't want to!

Why a chair, an antique French one at that, would want to talk to *me* made my head spin. Had I not been such a narcissist, I'd have asked the more sensible question. HowTheFuckCanAFreakin'ChairF'in-SpeakInTheFirstFuckin'PlaceTellMeThat?

An even more sensible person would have bailed—took a walk—hit a bar—called a f'in therapist! However, Evangeline had left me to watch the store, and those choices weren't in the cards. Instead, I didn't budge. I just listened. Oh, that's not entirely true. I did inquire whether MonseurFussyFauteuil ever had the pleasure of entertaining a RoyalButtski. Still, he brushed aside my question, as if I were a total idiot, and had asked if he would have been happier had he been born a Bergère.

I confess if the same thing ever happened to you—you can't do better than an 18th Century Fauteuil—especially one bursting with juicy gossip and ReadyTeddyGoManGo to unload it all when the Buttski sat itself down on him.

Why me? Why did I have the right buttski? And there, said the Bard, lies the rub.

WHAT VIRUS?

"What Virus, Bernie?"

I was floored. Maggie had Igor's 'What Hump' zinger and 'hunchback stoop' down pat. Thank God, she didn't have his bulging eyes!

I should have guessed. The twisted, humorous connection between Mary Shelley's *Frankenstein* and *Young Frankenstein* by Mel Brooks was too good for Maggie to pass up, so when we met at the corner of Eighteenth and First and I mentioned how deserted the streets were due to the virus, Maggie did the routine.

"I couldn't resist," she laughed.

I would have immediately answered; instead, I was doubled-over and trying to catch my breath from laughing so hard.

"Here, I hate to see a man cry." She handed me a Cotttonelle flushable wipe.

I pulled off my mask and wiped the tears from my eyes. It took another moment before I was able to breathe naturally.

I wiped my nose and said, "I don't want to run with Mucus," wondering if she got the reference to another great Brook's line, this one from *The History of The World Part 1*.

"Don't get saucy with me, Bernaise," she quipped.

And there it was! She f'in nailed it!

It was just two days ago Maggie and I met on FaceTime after connecting on BackAgain.com. I was the first man she had encountered who wasn't afraid to admit he once had been a woman.

"Bernie, you'd be surprised at how many guys are homophobic. I mean—I've changed genders a couple of times, no big deal. But you guys..."

Maggie went on to tell me that thanks to BackAgain.com, she had learned she was the reincarnation of Henriette-Julie de Murat.

"You know who she is, Bernie?"

I shook my head, "Afraid not."

"Well, let me tell you how proud I am to have the DNA of Madame Henriette-Julie de Murat. It makes me what I am today. This brave femme was a bitch on wheels. First off, she was a writer, and when she heard some dickless wonder had written a book in which he described women as being incapable of virtue and of being fickle, my girl took the asswipe to the woodshed and laid him silly. Unfortunately, that created a family shit storm and she was disinherited. Story sound familiar, Bernie?"

"All too familiar, I'm sorry to say."

"Glad to hear you're on board with me, Bernie. I knew you would be. Anyway, to get on with the story, taking away all her money wasn't enough. The family then smeared her by saying she was a lesbian, got the courts to send her to some scary jail with a fancy name—Château de Loches."

"Sounds more like a palace than a jail," I said.

"They don't call French a romance language for nothing."

We both laughed.

It amazed me to see how Maggie's caught up in this woman's history, and I wondered if I'd feel that same intense connection with Mary Shelley.

"You still with me, Bernie?"

"Absolutely! One hundred percent."

"Okay! So, she's in jail, but that doesn't stop her from living the life, having some fun, and what else—don't you know, she gets herself preggers, with whom no one knows. Well, that just cuts it, doesn't it? Confirms the family judgment—she's a tramp of the first class. But Henriette-Julie de Murat doesn't take this lying down, no pun intended; figures she can escape by—get this—dressing up as a guy! Why the hell not? She's a lesbian, right? Anyway, she gets caught; they send her off to a couple of other jails, but she's got friends in high places, is eventually given a pardon by the Countess d'Argenton. Now, I don't know this to be true, but I bet she, and this Countess d'Argenton, shared many a carnal pleasure. Anyway, Ms. Murat goes on to write fairy tales and a ghost story and wins herself a whole slew of literary honors."

"That's some story, Maggie. I wonder if her books are still in print?"

"I read all the short stories—fairy tales, and best of all her ghost story, *A Trip to the Country*. Want to hear something strange?"

"Sure, go ahead," I said.

"About two months ago, I started having dreams about Casper The Friendly Ghost."

"The cartoon character?"

"I don't remember much, but we do a lot of dancing. Weird, right?"

I had nothing but a nod and a half-smile because MeMySelf-AndIBernieMax was thinking: DreamsDreamsIDon'tNeedNoStinking MaryShelleyMonsterDreams!

Maggie had parked right off Avenue C on a very long and narrow deserted side street reserved for Con Ed Employees.

"I heard about this area from a guy that works here when we were shopping for Foresters. He said there were always one or two spaces because guys don't always show up. Just avoid the hours of Eight and Four when the shift changes and the street gets crazy."

Sure enough, when we entered the street around One, there were two spaces, one near the corner and one even more isolated at the other end of the block.

"See, nobody around for two hours, plus I have tinted windows—just in case—and get this!" She started to bounce up and down in her seat. "No movement! The car's built like a tank!"

We made love in the front passenger seat of her brand new, bright red, 2021 Subaru Forrester she had picked up from the dealership the past weekend. Tinted windows made us invisible to prying eyes (don't think I didn't check it out first), but it was the heated seats that almost drove my BoyWonder into TheLandOfScotaSoftness.

I averted disaster by quickly hitting the power window button, awakening my shaft with its shaft of cold air. This unusual and constant heating of the Johnson was something I needed to tell the BoysInTheLabOfTheBluePills so that they could warn users of the dangers of HSLD (HotSeatLimpDick).

Maggie was about to say something as she pulled down her jeans, exposing her PantlessPussy, but when she saw my StiffyShaftSalute she freed one hand, grabbed my throbbing BebopBoyWonder and we were ReadyTeddyToRockAndRoll.

As she moved slowly, rhythmically, up and down my Johnson, I found myself singing, "Oh Every Little Breeze Seems To Whisper Louise" in my head, while Maggie, as she picked up momentum, began twisting and shouting—"Oh, it's good to be the Queen! Oh, it's good to be the Queen!"

MAGGIE

She liked to be called Maggie. I guessed that was short for Margaret, a moniker she probably thought old-fashioned. If I wanted, I could call her Flower, the nickname her maiden aunt chose the moment she saw the tiny infant give out her first cry. I picked Maggie.

For our second assignation, Maggie kept the location a secret until she gave me the all-clear, and I left my doorway-hiding place, trotted the twenty feet through the open door, and entered a pet store.

"How cool is this, Bernie? I mean, not what you expected, am I right?"

As I looked around, I realized it was more luxurious than a typical pet store.

"What is this place?"

"A dog spa and hotel. If I told you how much it costs to put your pet through a day here, you'd have a conniption."

When I got into her car, I hadn't noticed what she was wearing, but now as she stood before me, I saw we were identically dressed.

She smiled. "Not to worry, I'm not looking to be your twin. We both happen to shop at Paragon."

I unzipped my parker.

"Don't get too comfy; we're not here to take advantage of the facilities."

She picked up on my confusion. "Oh, don't worry, I'm not going to ask you to get on all fours and bark like a dog." She gave me a

WilyEyeTwinkleTwinkle and GrinnyGrinGrin. "Unless that's what you want to do?"

I shook my head and tried to smile.

"Okay, then follow me." She laughed as she held out her hand.

I took it, and she led me into what looked like an old-fashioned barbershop.

As we both looked around she said, "Nice, right?"

I nodded but didn't have much time to examine my surroundings because she directed me to sit down on the barber chair, and within seconds had opened her parker to reveal naked breasts that she gently eased into my face.

After I SawStarsAndMurmuredIsThisTheEndOfBernie, Maggie continued to hold tight to my Johnson; eyes closed, wet open lips, a sliver of velvety pleasure exposing gleaming white teeth, making me think she'd be perfect for a toothpaste commercial.

Finally, murmuring, "Do you think Mary Shelley is experiencing your pleasures right now?"

Before I could respond, that is if I had a response, which I didn't, she continued... "I mean, if you're a direct descendant you have her genetic makeup in your DNA, right?"

After hearing such a proclamation, any ordinary Johnson would have hightailed it up into my abdominal wall before being taken prisoner by this nutter and her JawsOfInsatiableVaginaInsanity; but, BoyWonder feasting off the BluePillSpecial had his own agenda.

"What makes sense to me—and Bernie, I have given this much thought—if we have their DNA—then they are alive in us: in bones, tissues, every cell. This theory leads me to conclude since all is alive within our aliveness—isn't it possible—actually, probable they're experiencing what we're experiencing?"

She tousled my hair and said, "You just gave Mary Shelley one fuckin' great orgasm! How cool is that?"

"Very cool," I murmured. *Hey, the ManlyManRoot is here to serve, right?*

She gazed into my eyes, and TheTwoThousandWattTwinkling should have been a warning, but I, as she, were in the euphoric grip of chemicals.

"Do you believe in ghosts?" she asked in a voice that appeared to reverb in my cerebral cortex.

I felt BoyWonder stir, and so did Maggie.

She smiled and softly asked, "Remember, about a year ago, a groomer was shot to death by her estranged husband who thought she was cheating on him? Came in, shot her three times—dead— then turned the gun on himself?"

She pointed her finger at her head and said, "And boom—blew out his brains."

Oh fuck! My Willy nearly jumped out of her hand!

"Oh my, oh my!" She smiled, and then all I saw was the top of her head.

Real men don't cry; we just suck it up (how ironic is that), because even with an OhMyAchingJohnsonWeDon'tFuckin'Disappoint! Can I have an Amen! So, I GaveAndGaveAndWhenThereWasNoMoreTo-GiveIGaveSomeMore, and now that it's over, I just sat in the chair while she washed up and waited until it was my turn. I could only hope cold water would resuscitate the BoyWonder, its lifeless form I no longer rec-ognized. (UD or UnrecognizableDick, another side effect and another warning I had to give the BoysInTheLabOfTheBluePills.

Fifteen minutes later, Maggie climbed back onto my lap and resumed her ghost story, her cheeks a little more flush, her speech a tiny bit slower.

"After the shooting, half the clientele bailed. Then the pandemic and the owner bailed. It's on the market with my firm, but nothing's moving."

"That's how you got the keys?"

"I have lots of properties, Bernie... and lots of keys."

I could swear her twinkling eyes added another thousand watts of electrical energy that, MiracleUponMiracleThankYouLord, brought the LoveJuice flowing again, initiating a StiffyShaftSalute upon which my strawweight sat. As any stud muffin knows, the next move is TheEarNibbleAndTheYumYumMumble.

"Blow in my ear," she commanded, or was it Mademoiselle Henriette-Julie de Murat barking the order?

I MISSED THAT
DAY IN CLASS

*I*t started in an office building, and I thought, oh shit, it's the same old *I'mFiredAndFindingSomeoneElseInMyOfficeNightmare; but, no, I have a big- time job as an agent for a famous singer, and this is my window office. I'm attempting to tell another agent, my client's boyfriend, there are two ways to fall in love with her. JUMP CUT. We are on 57th Street, in front of the Russian Tea Room, and I'm continuing to espouse my theory. Sure, you did it the traditional way, met her, fell under her spell (his words), and wooed her; but for the millions of her fans, they 'came under her spell' through her voice and storytelling singing style. JUMP CUT. I'm in the singer's office, and now she's turned into my girlfriend. She's introducing me as such by giving me a nickname, only I'm looking at her and suddenly seeing a small, plain-looking woman who I don't find appealing, and I'm thinking, how do I disentangle myself from this arrangement. JUMP CUT. I'm with Jenifer Lawrence (before she's a big star), sitting on a well-manicured lawn in the shade of a huge apple tree. I'm reading her poetry, and with each word, she falls more deeply under my spell.*

I vowed to break the FaceTime connection if Gerry makes another LightInTheLoafers crack, but he surprises me and says, 'The key to the dream, Boyo, is the poetry. Jennifer is Mary Shelley, and you're Lord Byron."

I'm UberDazedAndTurboConfused and protest with a raised hand. "How can I be Byron when I'm supposed to be Mary Shelley?"

"Laddie Boy, can't you see?"

"See what?"

"You are still denyin' your Clownfish."

"Clownfish?"

"DamnYourLyin'EyesBoyo, don't you remember Clownfish Day in science class?"

Oh dear God, do I! I had anxiety attacks every time I blew into a pipette filled with some deadly chemical—scared shitless I was poisoning myself.

"Clownfish are all born male, but that doesn't mean they simply do without female counterparts. Rather, some—the most dominant males—turn into females, a process known as sequential hermaphroditism."

I could see he was reading off his iPad.

"OkayOkayOkay, so I was researchin' this shit ever since we found out who was livin' inside us."

I suddenly get cold all over—numb was more like it—a new sensation and not the usual ScaredyCatShits that gave me the literal shits.

"If you were more together, you would have been Mary, and you'd been readin' to—oh shit—George Clooney—OrOrOr—that guy in *Drive* we like so much..."

"Ryan Gosling..."

"AndAndAnd, if you were really tight with your inner being, Lord-Fuckin'Byron. FuckMeSideWaysToTheCemeteryOnSunday, wouldn't that be neat? You and LordFuckin'Byron readin' f'in poetry on da lawn in front of your HumongousEstateInF'inEnglandLikeDowntonF'in-Abbey!"

Gerry could see I was still unable to process...perhaps unwilling to accept all this information.

"Look, Boyo, I know we got onto this site to get some LickyL-ickySuckyWokey, but consider the possibilities if we have RedCarpetWalkersFromThePast inside us, Workin'AndAPimpin'—getting us the ole pus-say!"

His smile reassured my libido. Why wouldn't the promise of pus-say be a good thing?

"I'm not sayin' me—TheManWithTheManlyGoldenManroot needs a helpin' hand. No—not sayin' somethin' so out there and outrageous, but—I wouldn't have a true PussyhoundNature if I didn't take advantage of a little ExtraExtraReadAllAboutIt; even if it meant I gotta mix a bit of TeensyWeensyEstrogen in with my ExtraHeavyTestosterone. Would I Laddie Boy?"

His smile, a promise of AfterHoursDelights, grew so hot, it heated the screen and burned my face.

"What the fuck! What doesn't kill the ManlyGoldenManroot only makes him stronger—right Laddie Boy?"

I was thinking Gerry should meet Maggie; each brings along what, their Reincarnates? The foursome could write a movie script about an ItalianMuscleUpOlympicDiscTosser and a FrenchCrossdressingGhostWriterTrollop, held prisoner in an Eastside condo during a pandemic by a ScientistCloningClownFishIntoWomenOfACertainPersuasion. It would be perfect for Hulu or another streaming network. Do it in a foreign language, get international backing.

Gerry, as if reading my mind (God help the poor bastard), cried out, "You gotta see this MaggieMaggieDoggieDoggieChickieChickie again! At that spa place like before—only this time—oh, this is great Laddie Boy—this time read her some f'in poetry before you go down on all fours. WooffWooff!"

LISTEN TO THE DAYBED

I could never fall asleep in the shop, no matter how tired or how many times I would draw near a particular 19th Century French Louis XVI painted & gilded Day Bed located in the rear of the lower level of Île-de-France. Not that I wouldn't be tempted by its perfect length and softness and the temporary comfort it would bring. No, it had more to do with resisting the pair of Mid 19th Century French Louis XVI Bergères that sat on either end of the day bed. Each, in turn, urging me to give myself to Morpheus, so I might enter my dream state and hear from one who knows (the Day Bed) the truth about a certain Fauteuil à la reine that had been filling my head with nonsense. I'm leaving out the giggles that seemed to punctuate every other word that came from these two NoseyRoseyBergères who, despite their considerable age, were filled with childlike merriment.

Let me backtrack a bit. In previous pages, I confessed to the first time I conversed with French Furniture. Well, since that initial episode, a day at the antique shop didn't go by that a piece of furniture didn't try to sit me down or have me lean up against it for a tête-à-tête; more like they tête and I listened.

Because Madame Evangeline wanted to protect against shoplifters, she had cameras installed throughout the shop. This video setup enabled her to view rooms on a bank of screens next to her desk located at the front of the shop so she could watch visitors and me at will.

When Madame Evangeline was out, I could converse with the furniture on the gallery level, but when she was in, I could only talk to the pieces on the lower level and always with my back turned to the cameras.

Once I forgot my placement, and I saw that Madame Evangeline was watching me. My pores immediately initiated a GangesRiverOfSmellingSweat, and I felt my face redden to the point of MassPulpExplosion. Madame Evangeline threw me one of her kindly smiles usually reserved for when I called a loveseat a settee.

That didn't cut it. That didn't ease my fears of being canned, NoSireeBobocats. Her smile only provoked TheDumbFuckerNeuron to fire up. In a last-ditch effort to save my job, I said, *"Since you were always telling me thoughts were things, I told the pieces the good news. They're going to a wealthy couple on Fifth Avenue with views of the museum where they could look out and see where some of their relatives lived."*

If I had been in my right mind, YeahYeahYeahWhatAJoke, I'd have realized this is a person who read my palm, drew up my astrological chart and saw my future that included coming to work for her. Had she had not said the Universe believes this is a positive for my personal and financial growth? So, wouldn't such a person know I'd be talking to the furniture? ButButBut, I wasn't in my right mind, hence setting loose, TheDumbFuckerNeuron and 'the thoughts are things bullshit'. (We'll see where that goes later.)

I did not get fired, but the incident made me even more aware of her presence, and it never happened again. So—back to the story.

Remember, Monsieur FussyFauteuil with whom I had my first conversation? Well, according to the fine, French, Louis XV period commode in solid, carved walnut with gilt bronze mounts from Provence, France, located at the entrance to the lower gallery, that particular Fauteuil à la reine was a relative of the carved and gilded walnut Fauteuil à la reine, ca. 1690–1710 located in the Louis XV Room, "The Morgan Alcove."

Well, you could knock me over with that bit of info, especially when we had an interior designer come in the other day and spouted out some bullshit about it being a repro and not worth over two grand. I couldn't wait to tell Madame Evangeline.

Oh, shit, that wouldn't fly! I'd have to find someone from the Met to come by and give us an appraisal. An idea popped into my head. Lucille—my art historian/lawyer pal who knew someone at the Met. I'd call her.

My dreams of dollar signs are interrupted by Monsieur Commode, now coming to the point and about to issue his stern warning.

Monsieur FussyFauteuil believed he should be the one to go from the royal manufactory at the Gobelins to Versailles. Because of this betrayal, he's been in a constant state of agitation, and any reference I might make to the Met would be catastrophic.

A nearby Mid 19th Century French Bombay Chinoiserie Commode with bronze mounts and marble top chimed in with; "*Mon Amie. I've seen this doomsday scenario play out in other Fauteuils; these poor creatures have the misfortune of being created without a stretcher to provide support and are destined to collapse their curved frames due to emotional stress.*"

I had no idea why I'd been the one chosen to hear this story. But après Maggie's lectures, I've been giving this bizarro relationship a thoroughly fresh PrefrontalCortexExam (thinking out of the box as they say) and believed I should have listened to the Bergères and had a lay down on the Daybed.

I went over to the window and stared out across the East River to the Greenpoint shoreline. The waters were calm and, for a moment, free from all ferry or tanker traffic.

Had I had that lay down on the Day Bed, perhaps, I would have understood it wasn't the furniture talking to me, but my ancestors, all of whom came in contact with those pieces and were trying to communicate through them to me. OkayOkayOkay, I know there are holes in that theory. For instance, the pieces in the shop come from all over France and from different periods. So how could my relatives contact them? Wait—not all the pieces spoke to me. FuckMeSideWaysToTheCemeteryOnSunday! Shit, I don't fucking remember which pieces! Could it be possible? Could it be possible this is part of what the Universe had planned for me? Could it be possible that is why Madame Evangeline put me in the store?

I turned back into the room. "So, why didn't you talk to me about that, HuhHuhHuh?"

The Voice didn't answer me. I have a couple of pieces of Danish Modern my father left me, but they never said a word to me in all the years I've lived here, and as I glanced over at them, it was apparent they weren't going to start now.

How the fuck could I bury such strangeness? How the fuck, can anyone live with such weirdness?

I suddenly felt alone and very depressed. I touched my forehead. No temperature. I licked my tongue and tasted the saliva.

"No Covid for me. I'll try the white Burgundy tonight if you please."

No one responded to my joke. Maybe, just maybe, it was because I was speaking in a voice that only can be best described as Charlie Chan on helium—HuhHuhHuh?

WHAT GOES AROUND, COMES AROUND

"Look, I'm not turnin' my back on the broads from Back-Again.com. Not sayin' NoMoreNookyFromYesterYear—but damn—when a piece of today's pus-say stares me right in the face, think I'm gonna say no cause I don't wanna cheat on someone who died a hundred years ago?"

He giggled. He liked his analogy and continued, "You're not sayin' these ancestors of mine are like wives, and I have to stay true to them, are ya, Laddie Boy?"

"I didn't say that."

It was a murmur. My head was spinning; I was so confused. Oh, what the Fuck! "Absolutely, right on, Gerry," I respond with as much conviction as I can muster.

"Read my flappin' lips, Boyo. We can go in two directions at once. Shit—the dick—the ManlyGoldenManRoot—half the time he doesn't know if he's goin' forwards or backward."

"I don't know whether I'm going forwards or backward, Gerry. That's the problem."

"The way I see it, Boyo, it's like keeping company with two BabyCakes at the same time. Like someone you might be porkin' or have porked and someone new you've got a hard-on for. You've done that, right?"

When I didn't react, Gerry used the opportunity to unshame me by reaching for his Ocean Spray Cran-Pomegranate.

"Okay, let me address the subject from a different perspective. Right now, you, or shall I say you and your famous relative, are catnip for some LovelyLadyOfThePus-Say of similar duality, and together, all four of you are gettin' a little. Is that not CorrectoColonFull-StopInTheNameOfLove, Laddie Boy?"

"I liked the previous analogy. You know, Girlfriend from the Past vs. Girlfriend of the Present."

"Boyo, you had to be there when darlin' Lorraine from down the hall KnockKnockKnocksOnGerry'sDoor wearin' nothin' under a robe she musta stolen from a ten-year-old and lookin' as pretty as punch...purrs...you got any sugar—sugar?"

He giggled. "On second thought, glad you weren't. Not like that youngin' wouldn't have done us both."

I was blowing my nose with more regularity, and my sinus drip was causing me to cough intermittently and alarming Gerry. Before he could ask me the series of dreaded questions, I thought to relieve him of his anxiety.

"It's just a sinus drip. I can still smell. I still have my sense of taste. No fever, and like I said, the drip is causing me to cough."

I had been thinking a lot about Mary Shelley (or maybe Mary Shelley had been thinking about me). As soon as Gerry and I disconnected, I returned to my newly purchased copy of Mary Shelley's *Frankenstein or the Modern Prometheus*.

I was looking to see if anything in the book could explain when I first swam in her gene pool. Then I wondered, could French furniture be the connection? Yeah, go on and laugh, but I've read books about code breaking and what's the diff between DNA, RNA, and talking Bergères? Reading between the lines is reading between the lines, right?

OkayOkayOkay, after one of my FrenchFurnitureConversations, I confess to examining chairs for a piece of paper, even a blank scrap hidden in a crack or under the seat. I knew revolutionaries knew a thing or two about WritingBackwardsInInvisibleInk. I came up empty. Suppose I had taken the piece completely apart; would I have uncovered something?

I did discover one interesting connection. In Mary's opening, she writes about passion as the underlying reason her story could be true. Beyond that, I found her opening chapters tedious and uninspiring. Certainly, nothing to make me believe Mary Shelley would ever contemplate living and breathing inside my DNA or communicating, showing herself in an unearthly way.

I vowed to continue reading. But not right away. I had more urgent needs. Maggie. Yes, indeedee, Ms.Maggie, or MaggieOfThe-ThousandKeys, as I was beginning to think of this woman who could open untold doors of pleasure was picking me up this evening for our third date. As before, she didn't tell me where or what we would do, and I didn't press her. Whatever she was up to, I had to make sure I was ReadyTeddyToRockAndRoll, and that meant re-upping the meds so BoyWonder would continue to bring better orgasms through chemistry.

Oh, there was another thing, actually two other things. I had been getting text messages from the Twins who were desperate to meet up, any time, anywhere, now that they had the Caddy back at their disposal. They used words like ravenous and unbridled lust, even attaching sexual positions from the Kamasutra, indicating which Twin was doing what to me, usually at the same time.

I decided to leave them be for the moment and address the other *thing*, Donna457. Her messages came under two separate subject lines. The first, how much she missed me, although she wasn't as graphic as the Twins. Obviously, she had no idea about Meryl and me. The second and more disturbing message concerned Meryl, who has disappeared from her life two days after cleaning me out of my Hanky-Pankies. Donna457 was worried Meryl had intentions of harming herself and asked for my help in finding her.

I messaged her back saying I would be glad to help and made a date for the day after tomorrow, figuring just to be on the safe side, I'd need the next day to recuperate from Maggie.

WHAT ARE FRIENDS FOR

I've been up since seven, waiting on Maggie to confirm for tonight, and it's only nine, so there's no reason to think she's going to stand me up, right? Right! When my cell rings, my Johnson's so excited he grabs the phone before my hand reaches it. OkayOkayOkay, that's not entirely true. Actually, not even remotely accurate, as BoyWonder and I are still a little groggy from having to get up three times during the night to pee. OkayOkayOkay, I know a man my age cannot drink liquids after seven pm.

The voice is unfamiliar, or is it?

"Bernie, it's Luke, your next-door neighbor."

It takes a second for the NameRecognitionBrainware in my superior temporal gyrus to match the voice to a face, being two cups short of caffeine, and threatening to shut down my entire right posterior temporal lobe if I don't re-up asap.

"Luke, how's it going?"

"Ah, I had a bit of an accident last night. I fell off my bike and ended up in the emergency room. Dislocated my shoulder, messed up some tendons."

"You okay? Anything I can do?"

"I was wondering, could you go over to Lenox Health on Twelfth and Seventh Avenue and pick up my x-rays? I'll need to take them to my doctor who's over at Beth Israel."

"Sure—no problem."

"Thanks, Bernie."

Sure—no problem. The answer was automatic, involuntary, without internal debate, second-guessing, or thinking through the consequences.

"It happened in Sheridan Square, and the ambulance took me to the closest hospital."

"The white building that looks like a ship?"

"You know it, huh?"

"Yep. I remember on the next block down; it used to be the Women's House of Detention. Pimps and boyfriends used to hang out across the street, and the women would scream down at them. It was a wild scene. Always drew a crowd."

"I remember." Luke laughed and then groaned.

"You sure you're okay?"

"Yeah—yeah. The building looks like a ship because it used to be the home of the Maritime Union. Then St. Vinny's bought it, and when they went bust, Lenox Hill took it over. Thank God—only emergency room in the area since St. Vinny's closed. They were terrific, took me right in; everybody was very nice, professional."

I also knew the area because that's where I had my prostate seeded. St. Vinny's closed a few years later. Too bad! They did me a solid.

"All you have to do is go to the front desk and ask for the x-rays for Luke Jeffers. I'll call them and give them your name, give you permission to pick 'em up. If you could go this morning, that would be great."

"No problem. I can get dressed now."

"I'll be home all day. I'm not going anywhere."

"You need anything else? Food, anything at the pharmacy for pain." *I didn't want to say I had a stash—figured I'd keep that to myself. I don't want Luke to think his next-door neighbor is a drug dealer.*

"Thanks, but they gave me plenty of Vicodins. Don't want to take 'em; they make me nauseous and give me a damn headache."

"I understand. Just let me know if you change your mind. Call me on my cell, and I'll pick up whatever you need on my way home."

"Okay, I will. Thanks, Bernie. You're a lifesaver."

"I'm happy to help you, neighbor. You just take it easy. See you soon."

I hung up and decided to take a quick shower to revive myself and then hit the road. It wasn't until I was ready to leave and decided how to get over to Seventh and Eleventh that I first developed heart palpitations. I had three choices. The 14th Street bus to Seventh and walk the two blocks. The L train to Seventh and walk the two blocks. Walk all the way across cross-town on 20th Street to Seventh, and walk the eight blocks down. I sat on my couch, paralyzed by indecision. Which route would be the safest? I immediately ruled out the subway even though I had been told and that subways were the safest on the TV because fewer people were taking them and everyone wore masks. The same mandate applied to buses, but I had no idea how crowded they were. Of course, I'd wait for one that wasn't, but who knows how many people would be getting on before I reached Seventh Avenue? Then again, I could always get off, and regardless of where—it still would be more convenient than walking the entire way.

I decided to take the bus over and on the return trip walk because the fresh air would remove any viral particles that might have landed on my face or body while at the hospital. I was glad I brought a hat and sunglasses. Once I got out of the hospital, I'd remove both, plus my masks. I just needed to find a plastic bag to put them in.

I had more spring to my step than anticipated, and I reached First Avenue before I could say, HolyFuckAmIOnRollerSkates! Man alive, I was feeling super jazzed. I'm thinking, why? Then it hit me. I'm on a mission, doing something for someone, and boy was that EnergyForMySorryAss. Bizarro, right?

So I said, fuck it, let's hoof it! The streets were busy, and everyone was wearing masks. Only a few were doubled-up. As I said, I had an extra in my pocket for the bus, that I wouldn't be taking; but I'd certainly put it on at the hospital. I calculated how many avenues before I reached Seventh. Seven in total, by my count. It sounds like a lot, but I've done it countless times when going over to the Apple repair store, a favorite restaurant, Cafeteria, or The Grey Dog. The last times were for more carnal purposes, searching appropriate sites for my DirtyBoyDirtyGirlRendezvous.

Walking at a reasonable pace, it took me another twenty minutes to get to the hospital entrance. Upon my arrival, I put on my second mask and hesitated at the bottom step but not as much as I would have had to had I not made eye contact with a uniformed guard who, anticipating my entrance, opened the door to the vestibule. A woman in street clothes and another uniformed guard sat at the reception desk. Both were masked and had on blue latex gloves. There were no other visitors or hospital workers near the reception area, nor in either direction down the long hallway fronting the building. I immediately felt more relaxed.

"Hi, my name is Bernie Max, and I'm here to pick up x-rays for Luke Jeffers."

"May I see a photo id?" asked the woman. She had an inviting, lyrical Caribbean accent that made me smile.

"Sure." I fished out my wallet, pulled out my driver's license, and handed it over.

On the desk was a bottle of hand sanitizer. I sprayed a few drops on my hands while the woman checked my photo id against my face. She smiled, swiveled, and from atop a long file cabinet plucked a sealed preprinted X-Ray Jacket. She had been anticipating my visit.

She pushed over a sign-in sheet, gave me another warm, friendly smile, and said, "Please sign this, Mr. Max."

I returned the smile, signed, and she pushed over the sealed X-Ray jacket.

"Thanks," I said and added, "And have a nice day and stay safe, you and your family."

"Thank you, and you do the same," said the woman.

I nodded and smiled at the guard and said, "You too—stay safe."

"Yes, sir, and thank you," the guard added in his lyrical Caribbean accent, his smile so bright it lit up the dimly illuminated foyer.

I tucked the X-Ray jacket under one arm, sprayed a couple of drops of sanitizer on both hands, turned, and as I left, gave a smile and a salute to the outside guard. He came to attention and gave me a mock soldier's salute. We both laughed.

I don't know if it was Maggie's message telling me we were on for tonight and to be in front of my building at eight, or the second jolt of energy I received from the friendly hospital staff, but before I knew it, I had walked the long block between Seventh and Sixth Avenues and I was crossing over the avenue, ReadyTeddy to hoof it all the way home.

Common sense kicked in when I reached 20th and B'way. I hooked a left to 23rd in time to catch the M23. To my surprise, the big accordion bus was almost empty. I hopped on through the rear door, and because I was the only one in the back, I didn't feel the need to double mask. In fact, by the time the bus reached its final stop and my destination, I was the only one left.

I wasn't ready for Luke's attempted embrace. Besides the fact that Covid had made embracing a no-no, I was amazed at how someone with two black, half-shut eyes, one arm encased in a sling, and multiple bruises on his face could move that quickly.

Not to worry, my FineFeatheryFriends, even though momentarily caught off guard, my JasonStathamTransporterMoves kicked in. I easily sidestep Luke, proving you can learn karate by watching a movie one hundred times.

I'm no good with people heaping praise upon me. My face flushes, and I get sweaty. All that went away when Luke shoved a bottle of Dom in my face and said, "I know it's not much, but it's an '08, and hell, if anyone deserves to drink this classic, it's you, my friend. Thank you, thank you, thank you!"

I don't think my feet touched the carpet between Luke's door and mine.

FROM THE TERRACE

OkayOkayOkay, it's thirty degrees, and MrFrostBite's just waiting on your dick, but how can you say no to a woman who calls your BoyWonder a Sky Bolt?

OkayOkayOkay, so maybe the alchemy allowed my little head to put one over on my big head, but DamnYourEyesYouJealousSumBitch, when a woman with a hungry heart leads you onto a ninetieth-floor terrace—points to the full moon seeming close enough to touch—commands you to unleash the Sky Bolt so all the heavens could see your awesomeness—ARoseByAnyOtherNameFuckYeahBaby—you unzip!

And don't think I couldn't wait to tell Gerry!

Maggie was now calling herself Shamhat, one of the holy harlots consecrated to worship the moon, and was ready to be ravished by the high priest with the Sky Bolt of Niurtra. That would be me.

"Just press up against me if you're cold."

When Maggie lifted her black cloak with the red scorpions slithering down the sides, off-putting to anyone other than my BoyWonder, I opened my Eddy Bauer Parker and pressed my SoftAsABaby'sTushHardlyEverWornRalphLaurenIrishCashmireSweater against her CorrectoColonFullStopInTheNameOfLoveBareFlesh.

YesSireeBobCats, she was totally naked under her priestess robe! Her hands went to my fly front, and then the magic act commenced. BoyWon-

78

der, his Sky Bolt, lit by moonbeams, warmed to the occasion, and all became possible.

No, I didn't come naked under a similar cloak, nor required to lose my new pair of jockey classic briefs. Shamhat, the name I was to call Maggie from the moment she picked me up at my apartment and drove me to the underground garage, to which we took the Tower Two elevator to the ninetieth floor, to the time she delivered me back to my place, two hours later. This holy harlot certainly wouldn't let mere undergarments get in the way of what she had in store for me.

And no, I never asked if anyone had been murdered in the apartment, the foyer of which reminded me of the ground floor of Lowes 83rd with its two chandelier-lit, heaven-bound staircases. I was awestruck by such opulence and hesitant to move forward. Maggie—oops—Shamhat immediately took my arm and eased me into the living room, at the same time explaining the apartment was vacant because the owners now lived in one of the penthouse units they recently purchased for a cool 120 million.

I don't think the great womanizers of all time, those Golden Studs: Ali Khan, Porfirio Rubirosa, Wilt Chamberlin, Hugh Heffner, Beatty, and Nicholson, were ever tested the way I was; nor could they have serviced a lady so admirably in such chilling temperatures with the threat of a deadly virus hanging in the air like rust on a water main, as MeMySelfAndITheSkyBolt.

So, you can imagine, I wasn't in the mood to take any shit from Gerry when he questioned my performance, insinuated I received help from my Reincarnates or was still doing my Fuckin'AsDavidDuchovnyAct to gain access to their sweet spots.

It was my fault for making him crazy when I said Maggie wasn't wearing anything under her raincoat. Had I told him it was actually a cloak, while a difference without a distinction, it would have made him crazier. After seeing *The Lord Of The Rings*, Gerry, like every male creature in the Middle Kingdom, had a hard-on for Liv Tyler and dreamed about getting under Arwen's cloak.

"Always fantasized about a RealEstateSugarPieMama. With keys to the pleasure domes of the RichieRich, this BabyCake does me happy endings on million-dollar rugs, grabs my ManlyGoldenManRoot, and leads me into gold-plated bathrooms, for some golden showers! Tell me, I'm not golden!" shouted Gerry, about to have his own orgasm.

"She took me onto the terrace."

"There's always the next time."

"I'm not into somebody peeing on me. You know that, Gerry."

"I'm only jerkin' your chain, Boyo."

"Gerry, you should have seen the place. She said there were two apartments, connected, something like ten thousand square feet. I'm telling you when I walked in, I thought I was in the old Lowes up on 83rd and Broadway."

"Got my first hand-job up in the balcony from Leslie Shay. The only girl I knew smoked Luckies."

"I remember—tenth grade—Mrs. Mueller—pink angora sweater."

Gerry was off in a daydream, then came out of it and smiled. "LSMFT... LeslieShayMostFantasticTits."

I smiled.

"Wouldn't it be fuckin' wild if she was on BackAgain.com?"

"Anyway, you could find out?"

Gerry was calculating the odds, then, shaking his head, not happy with the results. "Nah—only sends you matches."

"Google?"

"Tried it—nothin'."

"Linkedin?"

"Nope."

"You've looked her up before?"

"Others?"

I could see he didn't want to give me any details. Suddenly, he shifted the conversation. "This Maggie—where'd you say she works?"

"The Bayswater Agency."

"Seen them on those Million Dollar listing shows. She's a big deal, Boyo. Must be high up there in TheScaleOfDoughRaeMe."

"Gerry, I didn't know you were into houses?"

"I'm into wealth, Boyo. Shows on yachts, private jets, exotic cars, mansions...and the eye candy! When you got billionaires, you know you're goin' to see some fantastic cuchi cuchi, Laddie Boy."

Again, he changed subjects on a dime. "Did you tell her bout me? Your best bud—da Italian Cocksman? Maybe she can hook me up with some of her associates, like the really hot ones?"

"Is that what you're calling yourself now, *da* Italian Cocksman?"

He gave me the GerryStareDownIntoMySoul. "I know that face, Boyo. You keepin' secrets from me, Laddie Boy?"

I was getting that ItchyTwitchyFeeling, the one I get when I just fuckin' blurt out all.

"What face," I ask, not really wanting to know the answer.

"Like when I asked if somethin' happened in that apartment, somethin' you're not tellin' me?"

"I told you, we weren't in the apartment more than to go in and out. Like I said, she took me right to the terrace."

"You didn't forget the WipeyAndDipey, did ya Boyo? Didn't get lazy, did ya, Laddie Boy?"

He threw me that look that said, AreYouFuckin'CrazyDoYou-WantToGetTheFuckin'CovidYouAsshole?

Ah, The AprèsLickAndSuckPurification! No, I hadn't forgotten. I went into one of the guest bathrooms while she disappeared into one attached to the master bedroom. I followed protocol, rinsed my mouth out with Listerine, shoved a Cotttonelle wipe into my pants, and ended by gently but thoroughly rubbing my Johnson. I used the excuse I had to take a whiz, but Maggie gave me that IReallyKnowWhatYou'reDoingSmile and I figured she was doing the same. And shit, this was faster than when I did it in a car, outdoors, or—FuckYeahADoggieSpa.

"I cleaned up—real good, don't worry about that, Gerry."

"Don't want you to lose your head...*both* heads to Covid!"

He thought that hysterical. His phone rang.

"Gotta jump, Laddie Boy, gotta jump!"

His words sent my brain into a tailspin, and suddenly I was back again in apartment 90/91 Tower Two, hearing the voice coming from the little French Chandelier hanging in the guest bathroom that took advantage of my pit stop to set me straight on a few things.

"Monsieur Max, do not be alarmed it is I, the Bergère. Upholstered in Napoleon Bee fabric, the one catty-cornered to the Giltwood console facing Madame Evangeline's desk; speaking through this lovely French Chandelier who so graciously allowed me passage so that I may warn you of the ghosts that live in this apartment."

Thank goodness I had finished my après sex protocol and had drained the snake. OtherwiseOtherwiseOtherwise, FuckedNine-WaysToASundayInTheCemetary, when I jerked my head up to see where the voice was coming from, my other head would have played GardenHoseWhipLash, and I'd have had to go to my hands and knees and do my impersonation of Mr.Fuckin'Clean.

"I do not know why Madame Henriette-Julie de Murat doesn't allow Maggie to reveal the presence of the two unearthly occupants who live here. Nor confessed to the spectral existence of the poor wife shot to death at her place of business and destined to roam the dog salon until love reenters her phantom soul and guides her into the rebirthing waters of the infinite. As to the madman who took her mortal life, he no longer exists in this sphere but suffers flesh- burning torture in the bitter pits of hell from which he can never return."

BoyWonder went into HardAsAFuckin'RockMode. Could it be this shit about ghosts excites him? Or, could it be BoyWonder had become frozen by fear, as I, by TooMuchUnwantedFuckin'Blood-CurtlingBullshit coming from a fuckin' light fixture?

"I have been sent to warn you about Maggie and those that speak through her."

The Chandelier bulbs flickered.

"*And instruct you to follow the one who calls herself Meryl, for she comes in rainbows.*"

"Bernie, Bernie, where are you?" called Maggie.

The Chandelier went dark.

"I'm coming!" ThenThenThen—BoyWonder and I limped out.

COMING THROUGH
THE BATHROOM WINDOW

"Gerry, do you think your ancestors can talk to you?"

"Don't fuckin' tell me, another Italian came to see you?"

"Not exactly."

"What exactly?"

"Inanimate objects..."

He thought for a moment and said, "You mean your dick?" He thought that hysterical and let me know with two exaggerated peels of laughter.

"No, you moron, not my dick."

Putting on his little boy voice, "Please—please stop playin' with me. I came, and I went..." He thought that deserving of three extra peels.

"Serves me right—gave it to you on a silver platter," I said with a shrug.

He thought for a moment and said, "Inanimate like talkin' Test-TubesAndBubblin'LiquidShit like in Frankenstein's lab?"

"Not exactly."

He furrowed his brow without moving his cheeks, and then his eyes lit up and shouted. "Electricity! You fuck! You been lickin' light bulbs thinkin' instead of some monster, its Mary's dead pus-say you're bringin' to life!"

"Gerry, that's vulgar, even for you!" I had to give the nod to his imagination, however twisted.

He gloated and, in triumph, shouted, "Lamps! Fuckin'Flickerin'Freakin'Lamps! Morse code from the LandOfReallyCrazyBitches! It's like her DNA's talkin'—sayin'—stick your dick into a lamp socket BernieBabyBoyoBubbie! Make that ManlyGoldenManroot glow like a motherfucker and LiveHardMofoLiveHardForForeverAndEver!"

He made a ghostly wooing sound that even gave me shivers.

"Not exactly, but…"

"I'm gettin' closer, huh, Laddie Boy? Like you're hearin'…"

"Furniture. French furniture, to be precise."

"Furniture!" His eyes bulged, and I swear, swiveled in their sockets.

"And lighting fixtures," I murmured.

"Lightin' fixtures, French furniture—that's beyond fucked up, Boyo!"

"I knew I shouldn't have told you."

"Wait—wait! Once, I heard a Corvette say to me—wax me, Gerry, wax me."

"Can't you be fuckin' serious for a change?"

"How 'bout your pillow, ever hear your pillow say Please-FluffADuffMePleasePleaseMaxFluffADuffMe?"

"Yeah, I hear my f'in pillow, but it says my friend Gerry's an asshole. No wonder the twins only want to see me and not you again."

Like a sharp stick in his eye that got his attention, his laughing lips transformed into two snarling scars. "You been in contact, he growled."

OkayOkayOkay, I might have grinned a couple degrees south of a smirk just to piss him off even more.

"What the fuck, they called you, Bernie? What did they say? WhatTheFuckWhatTheFuckWhatTheFuck!"

"They said when Gerry gets a fancy car and drives his fat ass across the GW, maybe—just maybe, they'd give him another chance at some LickieSuckie."

He scanned every inch of my face for a sign I might be fucking with him.

OkayOkayOkay, I couldn't face up to the GerryStareDownIntoMySoulStareDown and burst out laughing.

"Knew you lyin' Boyo." He stood, dropped his pants, whirled, and mooned me. "Bounce a dime offa it! And kiss my ass, motherfucker!"

SEARCH PARTY

I met Donna457 in Stuyvesant Cove, the pathway along the East River between 23rd and 18th Streets. It was a comfortable April day, with temperatures in the low 60's, so meeting down by the river was ideal.

The last, and only time we met, she wore an oversized raincoat that made her more diminutive and totally out of place on that sunny day. Today she was wearing fitted black jeans, a white scoop-neck tee, peach knit cardigan with black Merrell slip-ons, and with nothing to hide her figure, diminutive turned into a miniature J-lo down to every exact InchieInchOfCurvaciousCuteness.

She pulled off her mask, and I saw an uninteresting face transformed into one sultry and exotic. Her altering dark, disturbing eyebrows when she smiled squirmed like tiny worms, now turned into provocative brushes of velvet dramatically framing, accentuating midnight-colored orbs. Orbs that absorbed the sun's rays—reflecting them like bolts of electricity, commanding BoyWonder, even without chemicals, to bore a hole in my jeans.

Needless to say, I didn't give a shit she might be a launching pad for the virus, and so I pulled off my mask and was about to kiss her on both cheeks when a runner came whizzing by, and I instinctively jerked my head back.

She quickly put her mask back on. I nodded and did the same.

"So, how have you been?" I asked.

The noise from the cars up on the FDR, plus having to talk through my mask, and the fact we were social distancing, made me think I had to shout, but I quickly realized normal levels were sufficient.

"I'm okay. I heard from my younger sister in Orange County. My nephew just tested positive, together with four of his co-workers. According to my sister, he doesn't like wearing a mask and is a real Party Boy. She's thinking of telling him to move out but can't bring herself to show some tough love. Of course, he has no money, so that's out of the question." She shrugged. "No place to go."

I rolled my eyes and was about to say something.

"Don't start. He's one of those kids who can't find themselves."

"How old?"

"Let's see. Probably twenty-five. Actually, he just started a new career in Food Services, and then the bottom fell out of the restaurant business."

"What about her husband? He can't get the kid to be more careful?"

"Vicky's divorced. Father's been out of the picture since Kenny's nine." Donna457 gazed out over the river. "To make things worse, she's got to quarantine for two weeks, and that's killing her because she's a teacher and the kids are her life."

"Can't she teach from home?"

"Not in her district. All the schools are open. No remote learning. She's really bummed out."

"Orange County. Trump land."

"Vicky told me they'd never close the schools in her district, no matter what the Governor says. Sheriff there won't even enforce mask-wearing, curfews, any governor recommendations or mandates."

A blur of runners kept coming by, most not wearing masks, and while I wanted to turn my head away as they passed at a distance closer than six feet, that would be rude, so I forced myself to keep my eyes on Donna457, who didn't seem to notice or care.

I knew it was only a matter of time before she brought up Meryl, so I decided to break the ice.

"So, no news of Meryl? Messages, phone calls?"

Mentioning her name returned me to the last time she put her hands on me and kneaded my muscles into submission, so gently, so effectively relaxing my entire body, I fell into a deep sleep. One so impenetrable as to render me unconscious; unable to feel her hands stripping me of my Hank Moody leather braided bracelet in black made by Flongo; completely deaf to the sounds of her collecting all my Hanky Pankies and stuffing them into a trash bag; and finally opening and closing my front door and skedaddling out of my life.

"She won't answer my calls, text, and no snail mail."

I see the lips move, but I do not hear anything.

"She's done this in the past, only never for more than a week. I'm thinking of calling her sister who lives up in Vermont, but I don't want to worry her."

My hearing has returned, and I hear myself say, "No other friends here? Someone she might have gone to?"

She shook her head. "Too bad you never met her, she was really a very interesting person. You know, she's participating in a vaccine trial?"

My mind went to NoShitIGottaHaveMeSomeLand.

"She's worked with the pharmaceutical company in the past." She nodded as if to accentuate her words. "In Africa, Asia..."

"Doing what?"

I was half-listening, desperate to change the subject back to the vaccine trial. I wondered if Meryl knew if she got the real thing or the placebo? Ah, they never told you. And me, what about me—could I get a hold of some?

"She works for an NPO that focused on food distribution to countries besieged by extreme poverty. She helped develop assistance programs; you know, designed to reduce scarcity and encourage economic growth in developing countries."

It was crawling back into a corner crust of my brain. The talking Chandelier, the Bergère upholstered in Napoleon Bee fabric—Meryl—she—comes on like a rainbow.

"She could have made a ton of money in the private sector, but her mantra was giving back. I can hear her now saying, 'I must always give back today, always give back today'." Donna457 began to cry.

That cut it. No More French Furniture Talk About Vaccine For You Mon Ami.

I reached for my handkerchief, but she beat me to it and pulled out a packet of Kleenex facial tissues.

"I'm sorry. I just miss her so."

"I'm sorry I never knew that about her," I said.

"How could you? You never had a chance to meet Meryl."

Almost screwed the pooch on that one, didn't you, asshole!

Her eyes smiled above her mask. "I don't know if you remember, she really wanted to meet you...had a mad crush on your look-alike, David Duchovny."

Tell me about it.

She stared at me. "Not so much now."

What! I don't look like the Hanky-Panky Man!

"Oh, you're still cute, but it's the Covid; it has changed us." She stared at me. "Don't you think?"

I could feel my WeepyEyeTearsOfInferiorityAndInsecurity dousing my flaming orbs and recovering their usual sheen, so I calmly said, "I think you look great."

How's that for LamoDribbleDribble?

She just smiled, blew her nose.

That did it! Boy, did I ever want to lift her off her feet, whirling her around, and tell the world this is my girl. I also wanted to make love to her. No DirtyBoyDirtyGirlQuickieLickieSuckie but inch by inch, BlowTorch-

Tonguing until my ManlyGoldenManRoot slithers into her love canal and the entire world could hear her HailAndFarewellWail.

She was smiling at me as if she could read my thoughts.

Goddamn, I hoped so. If thoughts are things, please God make her wet.

A SHOT IN THE ARM

Gerry and I are meeting for lunch at Hane, the Japanese restaurant at the corner of First and 20th. We're sitting in a heated sidewalk dining structure that reminds me of a beachfront bar I used to frequent in Puerto Rico. The only reason Gerry's come down to my neighborhood is to see Dr. Williams, his chiropractor, who has offices two blocks from here, on 18th and First. It was Dr. Williams who promoted Inversion Therapy as a form of physical therapy that could help relieve Gerry's back pain. Since then, Gerry's been hanging upside down and stretching out the spine sometimes two to three times a day.

When Gerry first told me what he was doing, I went to the Internet (of course I did) and discovered when hanging upside down for more than a few minutes, your blood pressure increases, your heartbeat slows down, and there's increased pressure on your eye.

Naturally, I kept my mouth shut and did not react, even when he told me about another benefit. This one doctors didn't like to talk about (except Dr. Williams, who also swears by it); that hanging upside down sends blood to that part of your brain that increases your testosterone levels fifty percent, translating in nearly doubling your endurance, excretions and ecstasy.

Actually, Gerry's description was less scientific and more to the point. "If she dies, she dies."

By the size of Gerry's pupils, I always suspected additional therapeutics involved when he sees Dr. Williams, but I—Mr.BluePill-Special—am in no position to throw shade on anyone.

Gerry is maskless, but I'm still wearing mine and feeling a little self-conscious.

"Goddamn, I feel good. Think I want some Saki. Still two for one here—right, Boyo?"

"Absolutely," I say, now debating when I'm going to remove my mask.

Gerry waves a server over and says, "One Sake for me and you, Boyo?"

I'm looking at the server and BrainFartBrainFart; my mind goes blank.

Before I can retrieve a single memory, the server says, "Malbec with ice!"

I laugh and apologetically give my excuse. "Sorry. First time eating outdoors since the Covid."

The server smiles and hurries off, and I suddenly feel safe enough to remove my mask.

"She's got a nice ass," says Gerry as his hungry eyes follow her into the restaurant.

"She's twenty-five if she's a day."

Still looking at the empty restaurant doorway. "What do I always say, Boyo?"

Together. "If she dies, she dies."

He turns to me, his eyes quickly losing their glimmer as they get further and further away from Gerry'sFantasyWorldOfEndlessSexualDelights, and says, "So what you're sayin'—you want to find Meryl because she can get you into some secret vaccine trial? That about it, Laddie Boy?"

"What do you think? Think it's worth a shot?"

"You got this from Donna457, not from some talkin' piece of furniture tellin' you—you should go back for some DirtyBoyDirty-GirlQuickieLickieSuckie?"

FuckMeSideWaysToTheCemetaryOnSunday, I knew I shouldn't have told him about the furniture—shit like that always comes back to bite me in the ass.

He must have seen how genuinely crestfallen I appeared, for he immediately tried to put me at ease by saying, "Look, if you think she can get you the vaccine, go for it."

"Gerry, she put me through TheFuckYouOverBlender."

Gerry gave me a very odd look, then he said, "What a pity Laddie Boy didn't kill that vile creature when he had the chance."

"Huh?"

Gerry then shot me the Let'sSeeIfYouKnowThatOneGrin.

WaitWaitWait, not so fast, motherfucker! Then I got it and replied, "Yes, it was pity. Pity and mercy."

He laughed, and we threw each other FaceTimeFistBumpFuck-YeahAirSalutes.

I told myself, next time I play Gandalf to his Frodo.

"So, how you gonna play it with Donna457?"

"What do you mean?"

"You gonna do her or what? Shit Laddie Boy, you nearly came in your pants when you saw her, didn't you?"

TrueTrueTrueAsRobin'sArrowFliesInFuckin'SherwoodForest, but our parting was awkward, and I didn't get the ComeFuckMeVibe.

"Oh shit! You didn't get the ComeFuckMeVibe, did ya Boyo?"

I had to laugh. The fucker could read my mind.

"I don't get it? She was on the website, right. She's a Dirty Girl, right, Laddie Boy?"

I couldn't remember how much I told Gerry about my first and only date with Donna457, but I'm pretty sure I wasn't honest with him and must have made up a story about why I didn't get any. OrOrOr—I told him I did get the LickieSuckie.

"So what—you pork her lesbo roommate, and she's pissed?" His expression told me he saw a different explanation. "Hold on; you're not gettin' the LesboVibe, are ya?"

He twisted in his seat. "You told me you got a little *Somethin' Somethin'* on the first date...what's with that?"

OkayOkayOkay, it's coming back to me. I lied. Didn't tell him about the homeless man, me getting sick, having coffee, and getting the vibe she wasn't a Dirty Girl, walking her home—end of story.

"No! The lesbo thing was totally wrong. Meryl was a singles hitter, and so is Donna457."

I quickly put on my mask as the server came over with our drinks but not my ice. Gerry remained maskless.

"Thank you, honey, thank you very much," he gushed.

I thought he was going to reach out and touch her hand, and she thought so too because she pulled back so quickly; all Gerry could do to save face was complete the stretch by picking up a napkin.

She smiled and said to me, "I'll be back with your ice."

"Wanna bet she brings me her phone number?"

"Look—she's—we're off that site—can we just call her Donna?"

"Sure, whatever." Gerry lifted his Sake. "Chin-chin!"

I removed my mask, lifted my glass but only took a small sip. "Chin-chin."

"Still givin' you acid, huh Boyo?"

"Ice will water it down."

He smiled and asked, "I'm your BestBuddyBro, right Boyo?"

I nodded.

"Then what you gotta do is get right back on your knees and call MaggieMunchaBuncha and get us a MénageÀQuatre at one of her FancyDancyTowerInTheSkyProperties with so many f'in rooms, we can play hide the SalamiInYourMouth without ever runnin' into each other. LickieSuckie baby, LickieSuckie, the answer to all our prayers."

He threw up his fist, and we did FuckYeahFaceTimeFistBump-AirSalute.

Who am I to argue? Who am I to worry about the virus, or Desire-UnderTheElms for the vaccine, or fret about anything fucking us over, when Gerry the ManlyGoldenStud speaks so convincingly? HuhHuhHuh?

"And as far as Meryl is concerned, Boyo," (he gave me that grin that says I'mGonnaGetYaGetYaGetYa) and said, "she's *my sister*, my daughter, *my sister*, and my daughter!"

For some reason, my cross-dressing axon gets triggered, and I'm thinking opera—Cherubino—but before my movie axon can kick in, I know by that I'mGonnaGetYaGetYaGetYa grin that has tripled in size, that I'm fucked.

"Forget it, Boyo. It's Chinatown."

And there it is! He nailed our relationship. I was Jake, and Meryl was Chinatown. I would never be able to get to the bottom of the truth. I took in his ShitEatingIGottaYaGottaYaGrin and liked it. What else could I do?

Our food came, and we ate, not bothering to worry about the sidewalk traffic except to GawkGulpGlareAndFantisize at the lovelies that strolled by.

We continued to eat and have a second beverage. I was feeling very mellow. After sitting for nearly an hour, Gerry's back was starting to give him trouble, so he passed on accompanying me across the street to my local wine store and called for an Uber.

Despite being a little tipsy, I crossed First Ave, saw that the wine store was empty, so I thought it safe enough to go in and load up on Portuguese wines. I passed up buying a lottery ticket at the bodega next door because the store had two people clogging up its tiny aisle and two more waiting to enter.

I managed to walk home without causing any harm to myself. After taking off my coat, I thought about calling Maggie. That's when I passed out.

DEATH IN VENICE

I'm in a four-story Upper East Side Building filled with antiques. It's the home of La Belle Époque. The owner is a longtime friend of Madame Evangeline's, and when she closed her shop he took her inventory on consignment, an arrangement that proved financially rewarding for both. I am here because the Bergère, upholstered in Napoleon Bee fabric that used to live next to the Giltwood console on the upper level just across from Madame Evangeline's desk, has a message for me. JUMP CUT. I'm on a floor filled with imposing 17th Century armoires. The only illumination comes from a window on the other side of the room. The floor is quickly filling up with water, and I have the sensation the building is sinking into the ground. JUMP CUT. A blonde, which reminds me of a young Laura Dern, kisses me. A warm feeling of release overcomes me, and I cannot believe a simple lip-lock has caused me to come. JUMP CUT. The water is steadily rising, but that doesn't matter. I must locate the Bergère and learn more about Meryl and the vaccine. The only problem, no Bergère, only armoires, huge and foreboding, everywhere you look. JUMP CUT. It's Waterside, the building where Donna and Meryl live; it's sinking into a Venetian canal.

I wake up. Goddamn, it's the scene from *Casino Royale*. The fucking building is collapsing right into the water. Then I remember those MenacingMahoganyArmoires, doorways to destruction,

ScaryAsShitSilentSentinals that open and draw me down into the drowning waters.

I need to pee. I'm opening my fly. My tighty-whities are wet. Another dream? I smile. Can you say Caterina Murino?

I VANT TO BE ALONE

"You want to know where we're going, or do you want it to be another surprise?"

The nap, OkayOkayOkay, the passing out after lunch, hasn't reduced my hangover, or maybe it's the two glasses of wine with my Chicken Tikki Masala from Trader Joe's at Five, and now at Eight, I was feeling a little FoggyWoggyDoodleAllDay—SoSoSo—when I said *sure*—Maggie didn't know what I meant; PlunkYourF'in-MagicTwangerFroggy, neither did I.

She put the hood over my face.

As she drove, Maggie made small talk, chatting away about this and that while I nodded, maybe grunting, all the while I was pretending to be Liam Neeson in *Taken 2*. I'd been kidnapped and had to memorize every street sound, time every turn, finally, time to the second how long to reach my destination so I could find my way back and rescue Maggie. Rescue? Oh shit, give me a break! I was still half in the bag and couldn't expect to figure out the entire plot.

"We're here," she said softly.

Maggie gently led me onto the sidewalk and told me to wait until she opened the door.

"I'm going to lead you in, but I don't want to take off the hood until we get to the top floor, because what I really want you to see can only be viewed from up there."

As soon as we entered, I knew we were in an antique shop. You don't spend five years of your life working in one without recognizing the unique smell of high-end antiques.

The little bell that accompanied the elevator door opening was recognizable too. Long before Madame Evangeline consigned her pieces to La Belle Époque, if she was looking for an item, this was the first place she went.

The length of the ride told me we were going to the top floor. Maggie carefully guided me down a long aisle, and when we stopped, I could tell from the cold air that we were at the window. In my mind's eye I could visualize the East River to the left and directly across the street the white Moorish-Revival-style apartment building, so out of place amongst its Art Deco and Georgian Style neighbors. I knew what Maggie was doing, as William Morris had done the very thing the first time I visited his shop.

Maggie removed my hood. "See the window directly across the street?"

I nodded but said nothing. I didn't want to ruin her reveal.

"Guess who lived there?"

"I haven't the slightest idea."

"I vant to be alone," she murmured

It was a pretty good Garbo.

"No kidding?"

"No kidding!"

"You ever see her?"

"I always knew she lived in that building. People at the office told me, but until we got the listing, I'd never been here."

"The listing?"

"For this building, it's for sale. Mr. Morris just bought a building in Long Island City."

I wondered if Madame Evangeline knew, and questioned if it would hurt business now that designers would have to go to Long Island City instead of coming to this more convenient location.

"Come?"

"Huh?"

She flicked a switch, and I immediately recognized the fifth-floor tableaus Mr. Morris had so cleverly designed after rooms at Versailles.

Maggie took me by the hand. "Viens mon seigneur emmène-moi au lit du roi."

I know enough French to understand we are heading for the King's Bedchamber.

Mr. Morris had been extremely particular about reproducing this tableau; the furnishing included the fine brocade of gold and silver on crimson, the painting depicting the Gospels, the clock barometer, four candelabras, and of course, the close-curtained state bed.

"Wait here a moment." She pointed to the bed. "Sit, relax."

Her seductive smile trailed after her like a harem aphrodisiac as she moved behind a Japanese Dancing Cranes Screen separating the tableaus.

I must have passed out, for the next thing I know I'm Shaken-AndRoughlyStirred, ShieldingMyEyesFromHerSparkles while she's TalkingSoftlyLikeGarbo...

"A great love, perfect love, is an illusion. It is the golden fable of which we all dream. But in ordinary life, it doesn't happen. In ordinary life, one must be content with less."

MASKLESS BY THE RIVER

I can breathe again! Fucking has set me free!

OkayOkayOkay, I admit, I'm still a little self-conscious when someone gives me the disapproving eye, and that's why I'm sitting on a bench in Stuyvesant Cove, facing straight onto the river, and as long as I continue to face forward, NoProblemoS'llVousPlaît.

OkayOkayOkay, I did wear a mask from my front door until I got here!

The river is teeming with ferries crisscrossing the waterway; back and forth from New York City to Brooklyn and Queens, the Fulton Ferry Landing, Williamsburg, Dumbo, Red Hook, and Sunset Park, to name destinations that come to mind quickly.

Then there is the occasional tanker or barge, and every hour or so, the Sea Streak, one very large MotherOfARoundTripper that goes from 34th to Wall Street and then onto the Atlantic Highlands in South Jersey.

I'm at peace here, trying to clear my head and make sense of last night with MaggieAkaGarboAkaQueenChristina.

I have to go onto BackAgain.com; see if there's a place to write a review. I've got a whopper. I'm related to Mary Shelley, who is catnip for a woman related to a French Ghostwriter, but—get this News-FlashMadamesAndMonseurs—add a second antecedent, Greta Garbo.

NoNoNo, I remember, I cannot write that review. YesYesYes, I have to keep this info on the Down low BecauseBecauseBecause, according to BackAgain.com, members are allowed only *one* ancestor match per client.

Now, why is this the rule, you ask? I thought more the merrier, right?

Well, Maggie put me StreetWise, and now I will do the same for you.

"It's the Law Of The Universe that humans are allowed to have contact with only one Reincarnate at a time," she explained.

Now, I knew that couldn't be true after seeing *Séance On A Wet Afternoon* and falling in love with Madame Acardi, aka Margaret Rutherford, so I made my case.

Realizing she was dealing with a sub-sect of humans who believe movies depict real life and not the other way round, Maggie let me slide and said, 'the 'Laws of the Universe' are there for a reason, Bernie. Otherwise, everyone who has passed would want to reincarnate and assume the consciousness of someone alive, most probably someone who shares their DNA."

What a scary thought. I didn't want to be changing sex and or building a Frankenstein monster. On the other hand, I had experience with changing partners. His stuff was gone, but had the Hanky-Panky Man ever left?

"Bernie, can you imagine if those laws didn't exist and the Reincarnate overrides our unique selves?"

I didn't have to imagine: *The Three Faces of Eve, Fight Club.*

"Bernie, because BackAgain.com doesn't want to disrupt the Laws Of The Universe, they connect you with only one Reincarnate; no exceptions. Violators will be terminated."

Maggie lowered her voice, took me into her confidence, and told me the awful truth. "When Dr. Keys ingeniously created facial recognition software to open a portal into the ancestral pool and create BackAgain.com, he believed he complied with the 'Laws Of The

Universe'. Instead, he opened a seam, a leak so to speak, allowing other Reincarnates to sneak in secretly as well."

And now my FineFeatheryFriends, do you understand? Okay-OkayOkay? Oh, you want to know if I did the nasty in the King's bed with MaggieAkaGarboAkaQueenChristina? A gentleman never tells.

ALL THE ANIMALS
ONE BY ONE

I'm looking at the sky. As far as I can see, it's blue with lines of clouds pinstriping the air space. (FYI, I always dream in color.) Suddenly, a white streak, then another, tears the blue fabric. The slashes appear oddly watery. JUMP CUT. A low-flying commercial jet crosses the horizon. Steel cargo cranes jutt upwards, so I'm thinking the plane's flying over the harbor. JUMP CUT. Sky's filled with every type of animal flying straight at me... tigers, sharks, whales, even some prehistoric creatures filling the air space and coming right for me. This is some scary shit. JUMP CUT. I'm taking shelter in a concrete bunker. Unfortunately, the bunker is open on all sides, so the creatures are heading right for me. It's a terrifying image, but I'm not screaming. In fact, the entire scene is eerily silent. JUMP CUT. Someone's spraying a yellow gas at the creatures as they try to rush through an opening. JUMP CUT. Quick as a flash, my unseen protector reaches another opening, and then another, each time giving the creatures a good dose of the spray right in the kisser, and like magic, they turn away as if they had run smack dab into an impenetrable glass wall. JUMP CUT. I'm still cowering against a back wall as someone yells the yellow spray is composed of egg yokes. JUMP CUT. Three identical Dr. Keys, wearing marching band uniforms, are lined up in a row playing the saxophone.

That tears it. I'm up, sweating, and need to pee. I'm too lazy to turn on the lights, so I take it slow. I cannot get the image of those frightening *creatures, especially the shark and the whale, out of my head. As I relieve myself, I understand those creatures represent the Frankenstein monster/ Coronavirus, and this dream is a way for Mary Shelley to enter my consciousness and save me (and by DNA extension herself), by directing me to Dr. Keys, who has exchanged his pied pipe for a sax, and is leading me to the land of NoMoreCovid-19 by playing I'mGonnaShootTheShitOut-OfTheVirusBlues.*

I'm smiling as I shake BoyWonder, knowing enlightenment always goes hand in hand with a MidnightTinkleWinkle.

ANNUAL
IMPROVEMENT
AWARD

As I take my MorningTinkleWinkle, I'm thrilled the gift of enlightenment still surges through my body, thoroughly deleting last night's terrors from the dentate gyrus of my hippocampus; so I can now get OntoIt.

I finish the last of my three shakes and return BoyWonder to my tighty- whities. I realize if I receive the gifts of understanding and knowledge, I must take a serious look at my life, for it's only through introspection that enlightenment is actionable.

I give a look to my look in the mirror. Hair disheveled, dark circles under my eyes and parched lips. I begin the ask; *"How do I get to wear the crown next time I fuck Maggie?"*

I DREAM TRUE

"I do not believe my chiropractor fucked me up and gave me a slipped disc or whatever the MRI says."

I'm on FaceTime with Gerry, who is standing in the lobby of Hospital For Special Surgery, waiting for his Uber. This is the first I've heard about his slipped disc and his emergency visit to HSS. I'm full of questions but decide to listen and not interrupt.

"I'm tellin' you, Laddie Boy, I need someone to help me lift the Johnson; that's what's throwin' out the ole back." He giggled.

The lobby's a madhouse, and with sirens wailing in the background, I can hardly make out what he's saying.

"The fuckers wanted to put me in an ambulance, but don't tell me they ain't full of the Covid, right Boyo?"

"Right! Absolutely! Never get into an ambulance. So, how did you get to the hospital?"

"Citi Bike." He giggled again.

Here are some FunFactoides: Gerry believes public transportation is a step lower than stepping in dog poop; Gerry rents nothing less than a Mercedes from Enterprise; Gerry is also the vandal you see at intersections, threatening to jam an umbrella into the spokes of speeding bicyclists, thus careening them into ongoing traffic.

Gerry rides a Citi Bike! Instead of yelling that, I ask, "But your back? How the hell could you get onto a Citi Bike?"

"Boyo, if you'd seen the Tour de France, you'd know that being bent over like the Hunchback of Notre Dame is the ultimate racin' position!"

Gerry checked his screen. "Uber's on the way, 'bout fuckin' time!" He began making his way toward the entrance.

"Ahh...how'd you get on?"

"With fuckin' difficulty, how'd you think?"

"And getting off?"

"Couple a nurses."

"Nurses?"

"Yeah, when I got to the Emergency entrance, I sorta—um—crashed up against it."

"Holy shit!"

Gerry was through the revolving door, onto the crowded sidewalk, and saw his Uber squeezing in between a cab dropping off someone with flowers and another taking on a man who had a shoulder encased in plaster.

"Stay by the phone, Boyo. I'll call when I'm HomeAgainJiggety-Jig. Need to talk 'bout gettin' me SomeSomeHomeCareLickieSuckie, Boyo! HomeCareLickieSuckie, got it?"

"Got it, Ger!"

Hah, since when have I been calling him Ger?

I don't know why stories about people going to hospitals make me want to make myself a Spanish omelet, but hey—different strokes, right?

So, I'm in the kitchen, getting out the eggs, Vidalia onion (others give me heartburn), Brummel and Brown Yogurt (tastes like butter), and some salsa (lazy man's tomatoes), while at the same time preparing my mug of Dunkin.

OkayOkayOkay, I know enlightenment doesn't come cheaply, and the price to pay is WorkItLikeAMofo. Therefore, answering Ger/Gerry's call could be viewed as a way my DumbAssProcrastinatingShirkingSelf's just trying to stay in control a little bit longer, but

HeyHeyHey, you want to deal with freakin' flying sharks and other airborne monsters coming for your head the first thing in the morning? AndAndAnd, what's with the three Dr. Keys spraying vaccine tunes out their saxophones?

WeirdWildBizarroShit—you think? Nothing to FearFretFuck-YourselfOver—you think?

Well, I think it's time for ConfessionTimeComingToASoul-NearYou! I dream true! BlessedCursedOrJustALuckyFuck—I dream true!

It's Ger/Gerry on Facetime, and the eggs are just about done. Well, screw it! He's just going to have to watch me eat.

"Spanish Omelette, how could I guess?" He lifted his wrist to show the hospital ID band; then to me he shouted, "Trader Joe's Chunky Hot Salsa! Good lad, go ahead—eat. I'm gonna order in some Sushi from Hane."

"They deliver up to you?"

"Boyo, you oughta know, anythin' is doable if you got the do-re-mi."

I scooped up a mouthful of eggs, happy that I put in just the right amount of salsa to set my tongue on fire.

"So, Laddie Boy, I'm gonna be laid up for a while and gonna need your HelpAJohnsonASAP."

"What about the Michael Jordan of women's basketball?"

"Who?"

"Your LickieSuckie Star of the '28 Olympics?"

"She's suddenly disappeared off the site. I got a feeling she's got another HostessWithTheMostess. Well, fuck it! Her loss is my gain, right Boyo?"

"I can ask Greta, but I don't think she's going to go for it."

"Who the fuck is Greta?"

Oh shit, I'm going to have to come clean. "One of Maggie Reincarnates."

"Not the ghostwriter?"

"No. Somebody different."

"What about yours?

"Huh?"

"Your FRR?"

"FRR?"

"FacialRecognitionReincarnate!   MaryMonsterMakerShelley! Come on, Boyo, get with the fuckin' program!"

"Oh, her..."

"Yeah—her, Boyo! Well, maybe you should check the website. I'm sure there are more MagpieMaggies, just as crazy for your MaryShelleyMonsterJohnson. I mean, why else would they want your female Reincarnate unless she endowed her host—that be you Boyo—with a cast iron meat candle?"

He grinned, "Unless they were Lesbos and goin' down on you was like goin' down on Mary."

He burst out laughing until he yelled in pain, "Oh, my fuckin' back!"

Should I tell Gerry? The pings have been coming two a day.

I must have a dozen inquiries. Oh fuck, I must be blushing because he banished the pain and replaced it with a mischievous grin.

"Look at you; you're fuckin' blushin', Boyo! She's come out to play, hasn't she, Boyo!"

I thought it would give him apoplexy the way the fool was laughing.

"Like in *Young Frankenstein*—turned your Willy into a Mary-ShelleyMonsterJohnson!"

Funny, with all the shit going on about reincarnation, I haven't given a thought to my FacialRecognitionReincarnate. And no, she has not come out to play. Thank fucking God. I mean, I wouldn't turn down a cast iron meat candle (who would), but I have enough chaos in my life without Mary Shelley taking over the small part of my brain that's still sane or what passes for it in my world.

"No. Mary hasn't come out to play," I finally confess.

"Well, get to it. I'm layin' on my back, ReadyWillin'AndJohnsonAble to have some HoneyBunnyHoney sit on my face and play GuessMyWeightBigBoy."

I was beginning to see the forest for the trees, or is the other way around? Who gives a shit! What was important was to say fuck to the enlightenment crap. Shove the DreamTrueBullshitMonsters, the MagpieMaggieCharacterParade et al; shove that entire maddening menagerie into an irretrievable part of my hippocampus and concentrate on the new emails piling up in my BackAgain.com inbox. Focus—focus on the new Pus-say! Can I have an amen!

SO DO THEY ALL

There were seven offers of love in the afternoon, evening, even twilight, and just as Gerry predicted, like MagpieMaggie, these FollowersOfTheDionysiacDNA were attracted to me because I am a true metrosexual and revealed my Reincarnate was a woman.

I was surprised to read these PerfectoSemiColonFullStopInTheNameOfLove examples of the SeducerSapian chose me over the men who listed such famous Reincarnates as Louis Pasteur, Samuel Ashcroft, Ernest Hemmingway, Luis Buñuel, and the one I would pick, Porfirio Rubirosa. (Who wouldn't want their own PepperMillDickToLick?)

Naturally, I followed protocol, eliminated BiBodilySeducers, who had carnal knowledge outside my UnZipTheZipperZone, leaving three NeighborhoodNaughties to contact.

OkayOkayOkay, so I'm influenced by my love of the arts, particularly opera. So, I'm HappyJumpingUpHapHappy to discover LucilleR's Reincarnate is none other than Adriana Ferrarese del Bene. Known later as La Ferrarese, the Italian operatic soprano who was one of the first performers of Susanna, in Mozart's *Le Nozze di Figaro*, and the first performer of Fiordiligi in *Così fan tutte*. Naturally, she rose to number one with a bullet.

Number two was EllenaP, and again, DumbstruckGoldAsAGoodHedgeAgainstDickDeflation, because her Reincarnate happened to be Barbara Strozzi, the Italian singer and renowned composer of the Baroque Period. I had difficulty relegating EllenaP to second place for BarbTheReincarnate had other virtues besides her musical talents to pass on. One is her reputation as a leading courtesan of the day, and two—WaitForItKids—her VoluminousVoluptuousness that ThanksTittyTitty plays forward, ChestHighAndMighty, to Ms. EllenaP.

GodDamnItGumby—she's going up to number one, and I don't want to hear my mother never suckled me as an infant!

Number three to join the TransgenderBoogie was FeliciaK, the most intriguing of all my contacts because her Reincarnate was the 18th Century French explorer Jeanne Baret, the first woman to circumnavigate the Earth. What made that trip even more WildWooly-AndRightDownTheTransHighway was she did it in the guise of a man, as the French Navy didn't allow women on its ships!

My FineFeatheryFriends, before you all, throw up in your shoes, sure I was Moanin'AndGroanin'Bitchin'AndABarkin' 'bout Maggie-TheQueenOfTheQuickChange and how unnerved she made me feel. So why, MomboWithThisComboOfImpersonators, especially Felicia K, because if her Reincarnate could pull the wool over the French Navy, imagine what HoodWinkie she has in store for me?

I'll tell you what these Reincarnates have in store for me—*what I say they have*! And what is that, MesdamesAndMesssieurs? The *pussay*! How many times must I tell you before I convince myself, Huh-HuhAndHuh?

THE MAGIC LANE

" So, do you want to hear me sing, or do you just want to do it?"
My Johnson had no difficulty choosing, but I'm thinking if
Lucille's channeling La Ferrarese and I could be serenaded with a
Mozart aria, imagine how that vocalization would soar through my
ManlyGoldenManRoot? We're talking SonicSopronicBoomBoxO-
peratic stored up for years just waiting to be released and into my
BoyWonder. Imagine that!

Tell me, what opera lover couldn't wait until the fat lady sang?

"I'm just pulling your chain," smiled Lucille. "I can't sing a note,
but I can play the skin flute with the best of 'em," she giggled.

Before I could say I can work with that, she yanked down my
zipper and out sprang my Johnson, and like a cobra going for the
mongoose, BoyWonder found a home in the palm of Lucille's warm
right hand.

April is usually a busy time for the residents of the neighborhood townhouses. They or their professional landscapers would be
busy as bees getting the basement entrance all gussied up for spring-
time. There would be deliveries of soil, planting boxes, whatever else
it takes to create some of the most beautiful and exotic gardens that
delight every passerby. April is when the TownHouseBikerDude-
AndDudette brought out their fancy racing bikes, folding bikes, high-
priced hybrids and chained them up against the iron-bared windows.

OfCourseOfCourseOfCourse, that was pre-Covid, and because at this moment in time, cases, hospitalizations, and deaths are on the rise in the city, ninety percent of the neighborhood townhouses are still dark and deserted. The shadows of their basement level entrances continue to provide the safest, most advantageous (dare I say romantic) environment for the DownLowDirtyBoyAndGirlNetworkOfNewYorkCity, whose motto is: GiveMeEroticaOrGiveMeEnnui.

I'm not aware of Lucille's past experiences. But judging by this assignation, when a car drove by or the shadow of a passerby darkened our doorway, either she was so deeply enthralled nothing could distract her, or she didn't give a shit if someone saw her or not.

"Noooo, don't stop," she moaned, urged, begged.

I was trying to come up for air and managed to get a few precious inhalations before she used both hands to force my head down and my face back into her sweetness.

"Come on, Shelley'sOwnMonsterBoy, more tongue—more tongue and counterclockwise this time," she commanded.

The addition of an apple douche to her VaginaLovePotion-NumberEve numbed my lips, and the thought that lockjaw could set in was reason enough to push me up into a standing position the moment I felt her clit vibrate against my tongue.

"Ooh, so good," she crooned.

I couldn't feel my lips, and my calves ached like a sonofabitch. I would have collapsed had it not been for Lucille, who held me so tight it was impossible to know where her quivering body ended, and my trembling flesh began.

Lucille tightened her grip as an ambulance, siren wailing, raced by.

"Another fever-cough incident," she groaned.

"What?"

"The call over the EMS radio. Use universal precautions; it's a fever-cough incident."

I was confused, and it showed on my face because Lucille, sensing my bewilderment, clued me in.

"Covid...I have a friend who's a nurse."

Lucille gave me a smile that said, Don'tWorryNothingIsEverGoingToHarmYou. It's the same smile your mom gave you when she asked you to try her latest mystery tapioca recipe.

"Let's get Starbucks," she whispered in my ear.

Since February, it dawned on me that there was no place or time of day you could hide from the wail of ambulances racing up and down the street, yet today was the first time my partner or I took any notice.

Just as we reached Starbucks, a couple got up from one of the outdoor tables, and immediately Lucille motioned for me to grab it and said she'd go in.

"What's your poison?" she asked.

"Medium coffee of the day, no sugar."

Five minutes later, we were sipping our Starbucks and smiling into each other's eyes when she said, "So tell me, Bernie do you think your Reincarnate gave you immunity to the virus?" Lucille's tone took on a seriousness that put me on Defcon 1.

OkayOkayOkay, since we're sitting on the sidewalk—MaybeBaby—a little coochie coo is too much of a want even for a DirtyBoy. OkayOkayOkay, so I can live without a FootToWillyMassage. I'm also not suchaDumbAssRomantictoknowHandHoldingDoesn'tGoHandInHandWithHandJobsInDoorways, but DamnHerBigBlueEyes, her StraightOutHealthCheckChillPill was cold, Jack.

"I think that's a genuine possibility," I replied. *I can smile, look 'em in the eye and lie with the best of them.*

She smiled reassuringly. "I thought so." She reached out across the table, grabbed my hand, squeezed it for a second, then let it gently return to its resting place.

She held my attention with those BigBlueOnes. "You have the look."

"The look?" *Holy shit! Can she see the Hanky-Panky Man?*

"The look of someone unafraid. Someone who understands that magical powers are protecting you from the virus."

My Johnson stiffened, and so soon after, I'd come! Oh, do I love my meds! OrOrOr, could it be the talk of immunity?

"At first, I couldn't believe it," continued Lucille; "then I asked myself, why wasn't I getting sick or testing positive when I was doing the same things as my friends, neighbors—people I worked with?"

She had a job? It never dawned on me DirtyGirls had a job. I always assumed they were like Gerry and me, TwentyFourSevenAddictsInGoodStandingOfTheDirtyBoysAndGirlsNetwork. Could it be members of BackAgain.com weren't all OurFriends? Was it possible they aren't all LoversOfTheQuckieQuickieSuckieSuckie? Was it possible these members belonged to a mystical group? And it was me, and maybe Gerry who, thanks to Dr. Keys, have cross-pollinated? NahNahAndDoubleNah! Didn't Gerry joyously proclaim BackAgain.com was Dr. Keys' Brainchild-InPerversionFollowUp?

Lucille again reached across the table and took my hand for a brief moment. BoyWonder stirred.

Was it because I was frightened my Reincarnate was flowing through my DNA? That factoid could terrify the toughest Johnson, even my Boy-Wonder.

"You know, everyone one of us on the site is immune. That's called herd immunity," Lucille said.

It hit me like a hammer. If my Reincarnate could do that, she positively could be giving BoyWonder a stiffy.

"I'm not saying we should all get together, like in Yankee stadium, but wouldn't that be neat? It would be like normal times again."

"Would the Yankees be playing? You think they're on the site?"

She opened up her iPhone and showed me the screen.

"What am I looking at? Ahh, a Moose Draw."

She took the phone and looked at the screen. "Cool, right? Wanna come?"

"Where?"

"Nova Scotia."

"Nova Scotia?"

That did it. BoyWonder became even harder, and I thought, damn, Mary Shelley wants me to go to Nova Scotia and shoot fucking moose!

"My ex is from Halifax, and when we were married, I became a dual citizen."

I couldn't pay attention. I'm only focusing on what my Reincarnate has in store for me. Would she take over my mind and body completely? And I thought I was in the shitter when I became TheHankyPankyMan. HaHaHaHa.

"I'm a very good shot, Bernie. I don't want to brag, but I've won several first prizes in sporting clay competitions."

She again reached out and grabbed my hand. "I never come home without a moose."

Next to having my teeth pulled out sans novocaine, I can't think of anything I'd rather do than put a dead moose over my shoulder and haul it back to the car through two feet of fucking snow.

"Of course, we'd have to enter a lottery, but I was just looking up my astrological chart for my Reincarnate and me, and we each have Jupiter, Saturn, and Mars in conjunction. It's a very lucky time for both of us."

She squeezed my hand, and at the same time, I felt her foot nuzzle up into my crotch.

The both of us? You mean, the four of us!

THE BEAUTIFUL
TROUBLEMAKER

"A lottery for a moose hunt, I love it!" shouted Gerry, jumping up and giving me our FaceTimeFistBumpFuckYeahAirSalute as he took a swig from his Ocean Spray Cran/Pomegranate.

"I knew farmers had a lottery for sheep, the fuckin' pervs, but doin' it to a Moose...?"

"Gerry, you're one sick individual."

"Now I get how Trump felt when he entered the lottery for those EasternPromises. Had to have one of dem hotties, BetchaByGollyByGumby!"

"You know the NSA is listening in on every call, so tell 'em you're only joking about our President."

He looked at the ceiling. "I'm only jokin'!" He came closer to the screen and mouthed the words: "I crossed my toes on that one, motherfucker!"

I looked to the spies in the sky. "I don't know this person. I love my president, and I'm proud to be an American."

I began to sing, doing my best and perhaps worst imitation of Lee Greenwood ever.

If tomorrow all the things were gone I'd worked for all my life,
And I had to start again with just my children and my wife.
I'd thank my lucky stars to be living here today,

'Cause the flag still stands for freedom and they can't take that away.

Gerry joined in, actually drowning me out, both heads looking up to our unseen listeners.

And I'm proud to be an American where at least I know I'm free.
And I won't forget the men who died, who gave that right to me.
And I'd gladly stand up next to you and defend her still today.
'Cause there ain't no doubt I love this land God bless the U.S.A.

Our love of country settled and proven to all listeners (we hoped); it was back to trying to DiceAndSliceTheMeaningOfReincarnatesInTheLivesOfTheDirtyBoysAndGirls.

This is no small order, and if it weren't for Gerry's innate ability to get right down to the nitty-gritty, I'd have been lost in the sauce and forever tied up in my tighty-whities.

"You got your rocks off, right?" He smiled.

If my Johnson had hands, he would have joined me in a Fuck-YeahFaceTimeFistBumpAirSalute.

"And she wants to see you again, right?" Another smile, this one ToothpasteCommercialWide.

Another FuckYeahFaceTimeFistBumpAirSalute.

"So what's the problemo, Señor Bernie?"

When I didn't reply, he chimed in. "You worried bout fallin' in love with a moose?"

"You found me out." I laughed and felt some of my anxiety draining away and cooling my face.

"If she wins the lottery, and that's an *IF* in capital letters, worry about it then, Laddie Boy. Right now—job one—catch the coochie-coo again. You did say she could suck the chrome offa a '54 Chevy, right Boyo?"

What about the Reincarnates—what do I do about them?

"Hold it a second, little fella. You're not swallowin' that Reincarnate bullshit aren't you, Boyo?"

Goddamn, am I so obvious?

121

"Remember what I used to call you when we went looking for broads?"

I nodded as glumly as the kid who discovered Santa hit the road and wouldn't be coming back NoMoreNoMoreNoMoreNoMore. "The RoadWorrier."

"Yeah, the RoadWorrier."

We both had a good laugh, his real, mine forced; and then he laid into me.

"Fuck all! Just stop, *okay?*"

I nodded.

That was my SorryAssHistory. I was—am—the worrying kind. My only savior is distraction. Thank you, Gerry. Thank you, MrMaster-OfThePussyHound.

"You take thin's too f'in seriously. I'm tellin' you for the ump-teenth time, all this shit about Reincarnates is just that—ShitayTo-GetThePus-say, Laddie Boy—ShitayToGetThePus-say."

"I know, but you should have been there. Lucille was so sure she didn't get the Covid because of her Reincarnate. She's talked to others on the site, and they agreed, their Reincarnates have made them immune."

"Look, I'm on so many goddamn pain killers and muscle relax-ants for my f'in back, I'm lucky to stand up without fallin' on my ass. And puttin' two words together without slurrin' the shit outta them is a real chore. However, my nose still knows when somethin' doesn't pass the ThreeDayOldFishSmellTest, or in Lucille's case, TheDead-MooseShitSmellTest."

He attempted to laugh, but I could see it hurt, so the delight went more in the direction of a groan.

"Boyo, if you don't quit Messin'WithTheStressin', you won't have to worry about the Covid. Your brains'll just explode into a mil-lion pieces of BloodUglyTissue."

He stared at me. "You not havin' more of those fuckin' dreams, are you? Not able to tell what's real and what's not—huh, Boyo?"

I had to love Gerry fighting through the pain to ease mine.

"Talkin' French chairs, flyin' sharks, bisexuals who wanna do the nasty, then run your male ass down in a pimpmobile so they can dress up in your Hanky-Pankies?"

This is why I don't go to Group. Some of us just can't face the truth. No truth. No mas. Not me motherfucker, not me!

"That shit was so yesterday." I smiled, adding. "Cool as the other side of the pillow."

"ReadyTeddyGoManGo," he yelled.

"Ahh...by the way...what's your sign?"

"Excuse me?"

"You know, your astrological sign? Lucille was telling me she and her Reincarnate have the same planets."

Gerry was giving me TheGlazedOverIntoOblivionStare reserved for when faced with a sharp stick in the eye, he zones out.

"I was thinkin' Ger, maybe you and me, and our Reincarnates, all have the same—you know solar system chart. That would account for it, don't you think?"

Gerry didn't say a word. He just stared at me until his eyes closed.

"I'm a Libra..." *It just came out. It wasn't as if I was bragging or being a smart ass.*

He opened his eyes, smiled the LongGoodbyeSmile, you know the one you give to the dead guy lying in the open casket just before you get up and leave the chapel—that smile.

BAD NEWS RISING

I was getting my mail when I overheard two neighbors talking. They had their masks on, and because they were also social distancing, they had to raise their voices to almost a shout. When they said my upstairs neighbor was in quarantine because she'd tested positive for the virus, I felt a chill, half expected a cough, and when I felt my forehead for a fever, I was disappointed it felt cool to the touch.

"I'm going to start wearing two masks when I use the elevator, go to the laundry, even when I check the mail," said cloth mask.

"I hear the N95s are the best, but my son says you can't find them anywhere," replied cotton mask.

"I'm just going to double-up on these," said cloth mask.

"You like them?" asked cotton mask.

"I love them, and they're washable," said cloth mask.

"Where did you get them, Walgreens?" asked cotton mask.

"Amazon. Give me your email address, and I'll send you a link," said cloth mask.

When I got upstairs, I washed my hands, removed all my clothes, and put them in a plastic bag I tied with double knots. I took a thermal head scan, and then to be sure, placed my oral thermometer under my tongue for two minutes. No fever.

I took a hot shower. I went to the Internet and ordered a UV sanitizing wand, protective gloves, and goggles when I got out. Then I called Gerry.

We were FaceTiming. Gerry was reading, and I was listening intently. He was clear-eyed, clear-headed, and apparently off painkillers. I was pleased he had recovered and was his old self again.

"Landlords should alert all residents that there may be a confirmed case in the building and remind them to follow the health guidelines. Landlords should explain the measures that are being taken to prevent its spread (e.g., the person is following all governmental protocols for quarantine). Personal privacy considerations must be taken into account, so Landlords should not name the infected individual or identify that person's specific location without obtaining that person's written consent.

The notice to residents should specify that the unnamed resident is self-quarantining or are under governmental order not to leave the apartment and that safety procedures are in place for clerical tasks such as disposing of trash or receiving mail.

If other building residents inquire who the infected resident is, to protect the resident's right to privacy and to remove the fear that such person might be publicly ridiculed or shamed, Landlords should not disclose the infected person's name or apartment, without obtaining that person's written consent.

If a Landlord learns that the infected person is not following protocol, then appropriate authorities, like the New York State Department of Health and the CDC, should be contacted immediately."

He looked up after reading. "That's it, Boyo."

"I haven't been notified."

"Maybe it just happened." He smiled. "That's the hottie that lives upstairs, right? Goddamn, she's there now, layin' in bed—naked—sweatin'—waitin' on you."

"Gerry, will you stop! I could have gotten in the elevator right after she was in it. I could have touched the same buttons."

"Since you got it, you can go up and fuck her brains out."

"Damn you, Gerry, I'm trying to be serious."

"You wear a mask. You wash your hands after you come in, and you weren't in her face for any length of time, so how the fuck do you think you got the virus, huh, Laddie Boy?"

"It hangs in the air."

"How many DirtyGirls have you hung in the air with, huh Boyo?"

I had to think on that.

"You get the virus from them? No!"

But I was protected, wasn't I? I was TheHankyPankyMan.

"Look, this is the tried and true SmoothMoveOnASicklyAss. You bring her a bowl of Jewish penicillin from the local deli. Two—yeah, brin' her two. Then—then when she's finished and lickin' her lips, you CopAFeelyWheely as you pick up the empty bowls. It's all LickieSuckieLickieSuckie from then on in. Got that, Boyo?"

Then again, maybe I was fooling myself into thinking all is good?

"Time to strike when they're most vulnerable, right Boyo?"

HolyMolyWhat'sDaMatterYou? I saw her this morning! When I went out for milk, she passed me coming into the building. Maybe a few feet apart, that's all. We exchanged nods. She was white as a ghost!

"She was white as a ghost," I blurted out.

"What?" Now it was Gerry's turn to be confused.

"I saw her this morning, coming into the building. She was white as a ghost," I said.

"Seein' you in the mornin' can do that." He laughed.

I liked him better when he was on pain meds.

"You were outside, and she wasn't in your face, breathin' down your throat."

"You get it by inhaling..."

"In the nose, the mouth, what's the diff? Get your shit together and get me a date with the one that sees real ghosts."

"Maggie..."

"Unless you wanna hook me up with the MooseHuntress? You know, Laddie Boy, I used to shoot skeet."

"Lucille!"

I saw he was ready to imitate one of our favorite rockers, so I put up my hand and yelled, "No—Little Richard!"

"How about "Good Golly Miss Molly?"

We threw each other FaceTimeFistBumpFuckYeahAirSalute.

"Speaking of skeet shooing, didn't you give yourself a black eye?" I grinned, remembering his cry for help.

"I bruised my shoulder, dick head. As I recall, you never left the clubhouse." He started laughing... "You had the shits."

"You brought Harriet. I thought she was going to shoot me; she was so pissed I asked for a divorce. She was more upset than my ex-to-be."

"You were readin' that fruitcake, Hemmingway. The story about the wife, shootin' her husband out on safari, wasn't it? How many times I tell you, TooMuchKnowledgeWillFuckWithYourBowels."

"If you remember, there was a shooting accident at that very club. Guy shot his best friend."

"Why worry, Boyo? My best friend's my Johnson!"

He laughed, but I couldn't fake it.

"Wasn't TheMooseHuntress the one who told you, if you're on BackAgain.com, you won't get the virus?"

That was true. That's what Lucille said, didn't she? We were protected. Our Reincarnates protect us. WhyFlushMyCheeksThankYouLord!

"I told you that, right?" I was convincing Gerry at the same time I was convincing myself." I continued... "She said it was herd immunity."

He raised his hand, and we gave each other another FuckYeah-FaceTimeFistBumpAirSalute.

I was feeling less anxious. Something about fist bumping, something I read about physical activity reducing your stress level—the releasing of endorphins or exciting the dopamine receptors, or maybe none of the above.

"Lucille said if you and your Reincarnate have the same astrological chart, NoWayNoHowOnGod'sGreenEarthYouGetTheVirusBaby, but damn—I can't remember where I put the chart Madame Evangeline drew up for me. You wouldn't know, would you, Gerry?"

I should have realized any mention of astrology would bring another LongGoodBySmile, but Gerry surprised me. NoNoNoAndNo—Gerry wasn't thinking about saying goodbye to some guy (me) in an open casket. NoNoNoAndNo, he was going to go Full-SarcasticOnMyAss.

"Sure, Boyo, I can help. Look where you put all your pacifier shit. That way, you could go FullCovidProtectMyAss by wrappin' yourself up in your BlankieWankie while sucking on your StinkyBinky. What say you to that, Laddie Boy?"

And this is what I have to deal with...

CONJUNCTION JUNCTION

I'm in a backyard, surrounded by a group of strangers. They wear the clothes of immigrants passing through Ellis Island. The children are cherubic, and the girls wear deep red lipstick. Silence. Everyone's watching me. None in that group wears a mask. I'm wearing one because I feel my heaving breathing coming back onto my face. I'm with an unidentifiable masked-up female companion of no discernable age. She informs me we're waiting for my blind date. JUMP CUT. I'm on a street lined with brownstones and trees, reminiscent of my childhood. A woman approaches. Maskless, white as a sheet, she's styling in a light blue dress with a jacket featuring a white clamshell design, an outfit reminiscent of the Hunger Games. Her plastic heels are so high I'm afraid she'll lose her balance and fall to the sidewalk. JUMP CUT. My female companion holds a motorized solar system model in one hand, the planets spinning round and round. She smiles at my date and reaches out to her with the other hand, and they shake. The women have identical tattoos on their wrists. It's the Zodiac symbol for Libra. They turn to me, and my date reaches for my hand. It's Madame Evangeline!

Suddenly, my iPhone buzzes, and the dream evaporates into the dust particles hanging in the morning light. It's a text. It's my health care provider offering me a health kit, including three N95 masks. No, it's not coming from them. It's from Gerry, who shares the same plan as I have.

I feel a shortness of breath. I inhale-exhale-inhale-exhale. I reach for my pulse oximeter—96 over 78. Talk about the power of suggestion. TrueConfessionsTimeYessireeBobCats. TrueTrueTrueA-sRobin'sArrowFliesInFuckin'SherwoodForest, I have always been influenced by the power of suggestion because my mind immediately anticipates BadMoonComing. Or, as the Old Testament so elegantly describes it: UglyUglierUgliestThoughts begat UglyUglierUgliest-Behaviors begat a BadShitShowComingToABrainPanInYourNeighborhood.

I checked the oximeter a second time, and the same results were no more chest tightening or shortness of breath.

Before I can check my email, Gerry shoots me another text. He wants to know if I've contacted Maggie. I put the phone down on the table and stared at my naked wrist.

BE AFRAID,
BE VERY AFRAID

Defeat, impoverishment, and devastation. I read that somewhere, or maybe I heard it at one of the governor's or the mayor's daily briefings, however, I don't think either of them ever launched into such eloquent perorations. Perorations, now there is a College Board word that has always stuck in my mind. Whenever I use it instead of a more familiar synonym like concluding or end, Gerry would say, "Now Boyo, that's a five-dollar word coming from a ten-cent dictionary."

WellHitMeUpsideMyHeadWithABaseballBat, after riding the M23 wearing two freakin' sets of masks that made it almost impossible to breathe, and hearing conversations, coming and going, about loved ones, friends, and co-workers dying of the Covid-19, what else is there but defeat, impoverishment, and devastation?

OkayOkayOkay, as soon as I got into my apartment, I removed my clothes—UV 'em —showered—no reason to panic. Right? Right! So, why is my heart racing? I take my BP—122/72. I pull out my pulse oximeter—96/71. I know those are good readings, but I go to WebMD to check out the numbers anyway.

Defeat, impoverishment, and devastation. So why can't I get those three words out of my head? What am I missing? What am I forgetting?

I was sitting on a seat parallel to the back exit, so I got air from the outside when the bus stopped and let passengers off and on. I'm able to choose that seat because 20th and Ave C is the first stop on its westward journey. OkayOkayOkay, the bus didn't remain empty for long, and by the time I got off, it was half full but, I still got the air coming in, and that helped, right? Right!

It was the couple behind me who got on, at 23rd and First. Damn— now I remember. As soon as they took their seats behind me, they started in with their lamentations. The conversation was difficult to hear, because like everyone on the bus, they were required to be masked up, but the gist of it was their relative had flown in from England, and a few days later, she was on a respirator and a week after she was dead. And only forty-six. That was the number that stuck with me. Oh, yeah, and she was a health nut—a vegetarian.

On my return trip, the bus was already a third filled when I boarded at 23rd and Seventh, and unless I chose to stand, which I was too tired to do, I was nowhere near an exit and had to take my chances.

ButButBut—it was the woman on the phone! She was standing right next to me, talking twice as loud because of her mask, so it was impossible not to hear she lost her husband to Covid and wasn't allowed to be by his bedside and had to settle for standing outside on the street below his window, holding up signs declaring her love and good wishes. She couldn't take it anymore, and she is thinking of suicide. She was on speakerphone, so the other passengers and I could hear both sides of the conversation. It was a co-worker, and she was pleading, begging for my fellow passenger not to do anything rash. She had a family to think of... her son, her grand-daughter.

I usually get pissed-off when confronted with people talking on the phone, sometimes so loud and annoying, I give them TheI'dLikeToTearY-ourThroatOutStareDown. If that doesn't work, I've gotten off the bus just to get my blood pressure down to BelowStrokeLevel and waited for the next one. But here, now.

OkayOkayOkay, like everyone else in earshot, I was frightened by the raw emotion and afraid at any moment, this distraught woman might harm herself. People were starting to give up their seats and move as far away as possible, even if they had to stand shoulder to shoulder with fellow passengers. I slowly moved away as well, and when we got to First Avenue, I got off two stops early. Not only did I want to get away from the woman, but I needed the fresh air, air that would wipe away any virus that had moved through the bus and settled on my mask or clothing.

Be careful what you wish for. As I walk through Peter Cooper Village, a nice breezy breeze and no one is around, so I remove my mask. I turn a corner, and two EMTs are rolling a gurney across my path toward a city ambulance.

I freeze and cannot help but look at the man on the gurney—an oxygen mask affixed to his deathly white skin. He turns his head, and our eyes lock. It's Owen Hirsh. I have known him for as long as I've been living here. We talk Ranger's Hockey.

I lift a hand in greeting, smile, and nod—my way of saying things are going to be all right. His eyes flicker and then he's gone, being lifted into the rear of the ambulance. I realize I'm not wearing my mask, and I quickly put it on.

Defeat, impoverishment, and devastation. NoShitSherlock.

BETTER CALL
MADAME EVANGELINE

It took me the better part of an hour to locate Madame Evangeline's home number in Columbia, South Carolina. I dedicated the first fifteen minutes going over contact numbers on all my devices. When I say going over, I mean OverAndOverAndOverAndOver. Let's face it, my FineFeatheryFriends, where else do you put phone numbers...because if they aren't there, they're nowhere?

"Hello, I'm Bernard Max, and I'd like to speak to Evangeline Morris, please."

"Who did you say you were, sir?" The woman had a thick southern accent, much more pronounced than Madame Evangeline's, even when she met a fellow southerner and reverted to her South Carolinian accent.

"Bernard Max. I used to work for Madame Evangeline, I mean Ms. Evangeline Morris, at Île-de-France—her antique shop in New York City."

Silence. I visualized a refined Southern Lady standing ramrod tall in a parlor, the phone in one hand, the other arranging flowers in an ornate vase. Roses? No something white? Tulips, Gardenias, Irises come to mind. Madame Evangeline always liked to have them in the shop.

"Bernard Max! Why, of course! You're that charming gentleman who so graciously drove us around Manhattan when we all came up to visit."

"You're..."

"Elizabeth-Rose—Evangeline's sister."

It all came back to me. Elizabeth-Rose, husband Carl Jr., and the third sister, Sue-Ellen, were happy first-time visitors to the Big Apple and full of fun and frolic. I was their tour guide, ending up at the observation deck of the World Trade Center. It was a clear day, and the view was breathtaking. Madame Evangeline's family told me how lucky I was to live in a city where such a fantastic view was available and how they envied Evangeline for living here. I didn't want to spoil their illusion and confess; I never took advantage of this magical city. Like so many blasé New Yorkers, I never visited the equally outrageous view from the observation deck of the Empire State Building. I never rode the Staten Island Ferry for an up-close-and-personal look at the Statue of Liberty. I was always too busy to take in the host of one-of-a-kind attractions drawing millions of tourists yearly to the Big Apple. What's the saying, 'Shoemaker's kids always go shoeless'?

"We were truly heartbroken to see the Twin Towers destroyed and just a month after we left! Mercifully, you and Evangeline weren't down there that morning."

Damn! I'd blocked that out! Just as I blocked out the weeks, months of living in a city that seemed to die along with those three thousand souls that perished that September day.

"We were lucky," I mumbled. So lost in the sauce, I couldn't comprehend what came next.

"Bernard, I'm so sorry to tell you, my beautiful sister, Evangeline passed last week."

When my synapses finally made the connection and fired off millions of BadNewsNeurons, I felt faint and nauseous.

"Bernard, it's so strange you called. I have your number in front of me, and I was going to call you—this very afternoon."

135

I had nothing. I just listened.

"There is a letter."

"A letter?"

"It is addressed to you, Bernard."

"What does it say?"

"Bernard, it is addressed to you."

"Oh, right. But if you want, you can open it, read it to me over the phone..." I left the invitation hanging in the air, hoping she'd take advantage of the offer.

"Oh dear, that wouldn't be proper, would it? Evangeline addressed the latter to you."

OkayOkayOkayOkay! I got it! Evangeline addressed the letter to me.

I sensed Elizabeth-Rose was holding back tears. "I apologize. Of course, you're right. Since the pandemic, I—I haven't been thinking clearly."

Why am I talking about my problems? The woman just lost her sister. DamnMyEyes!

I regained my SenseOfSayingTheRightThingInAwkwardSituations and asked, "Elizabeth-Rose, how are you and Carl Jr. and Sue-Ellen doing?"

"I lost Carl Jr. several years back, but Sue-Ellen and I are surviving. I do appreciate your concern."

Obviously, I had not regained my SenseOfSayingTheRightThingInAwkwardSituations, so I went into my HumblingMyselfInAwkwardSituationsMode and said, "Evangeline never told me. I am so sorry. I would have called, come down. I only spent a long weekend with you guys, but you were so kind to me. It sounds crazy, but in that short time I began to think of you as family. I pestered your sister to call, even take a road trip, but it never happened."

"Oh, that is so kind of you to say. It was mutual, you know. Carl Jr. always talked about you, New York, and how nice you were to drive us around the city and be our tour guide for that weekend."

DamnMyEyes! IGotNoSenseOfAnything! I shouldn't have said that stuff about Madame Evangeline. She had her reasons and didn't have to explain why she kept her family at arm's length—no reason to talk ill of the dead. Besides, I was too lazy to reach out to them, and it was on me for allowing the years to go by without any meaningful communication. This conversation is just going sideways. I just can't help saying the wrong f'in thing.

"Bernard, I need your address if I'm to send you the letter."

WELL, MY BOSS,
SHE WROTE ME A LETTER

Dear Bernard

If you are reading this, you know I have passed. Please do not be sad, for I am leaving the Planet of The Sorrowful Star for the celestial glory of eternal life. Bernard, remember I drew your astrological chart. While you may be apprehensive, I know what you are capable of. I know you have the strength and the courage to carry out my instructions. On April 19th, you will accept Maggie's invitation and accompany her to The Sun High, Apartment 90/91, Tower Two. Upon arrival, you will excuse yourself and enter the guest bathroom and wait. Bernard, you are already accustomed to communicating with the spirit world. (Of course, I knew); however, unlike the Reincarnate who connected with you through a Bergère, this Reincarnate will appear as an apparition (a less scary word for a ghost); nevertheless, a ghost is what it is, and a ghost is what I am! The adventure begins. Bernard, this is your destiny.

Forever, Madame Evangeline.

It's a good thing I had a couple of glasses of vino; otherwise, my first impulse would have been to tear the f'in letter up into a thousand pieces and then laugh myself SillyWillySillySupid. Let's face it, BoysAndGirlsWhoLiveInTheRealFuckin'World, if Madame Evangeline knew so damn much about my destiny, she wouldn't have written the fuckin' letter BecauseBecauseBecause—FuckMeSideWaysToTheCemeteryOnSunday—she'd have known it would arrive *after* the 19th—now wouldn't she?

Fortune smiles on those who have a high tolerance for vino and therefore in complete control after a glass and a half, and ThereforeTherefore, I reacted in a mature, adult fashion that would have made Madame Evangeline proud.

"Gerry, stop dancing around the fuckin' room and put the fuckin' Ocean Spray away and sit the fuck down and listen!"

I could tell by the flow of purple spritz that came spraying out his mouth; he knew who was the adult in the room.

"Now, I want you to read this fuckin' letter and see if it's written in code!"

It was as if I'd attached electrodes to his privates; the transformation was instantaneous. Gerry immediately knew the slightest hesitation or deviation from my orders would cause excruciating pain to every nerve ending in his ManlyGoldenManRoot until his PreciousPenis could no longer stand the agony and passed over into DeadDickHanging.

THE PIGPEN CIPHER

OkayOkayOkay, so maybe binge-watching *Curse of The Blind Dead* and *Vril* made Gerry dye his eyebrows purple, but it matched the Ocean Spray he drank during the marathon, and he did learn a secret code.

I sat in StomachTurningRectalKnottingAnticipation. If anyone could decipher the letter and work out its real meaning, Gerry was da Man. I mean, it had to have another message, right? Right!

A thousand-watt bulb lit up Gerry's helium-bloated cheeks. "Gotcha, motherfucker!"

"You decoded the letter?" I couldn't believe he got it so fast.

"Got to hand it to these mofos, Laddie Boy. It's so simple, a kid with sixth-grade geometry could come up with it, exchanging letters for symbols and placin''em like fragments in a grid."

"Tell me, Gerry, tell me!"

Unfortunately, it wasn't going to be that easy because ProfessorI'mTheFuckin'SmartestGuyInTheRoomGerry was just getting started.

"Watch and learn Boyo, watch and learn how the Knights Templar came up with the Pig-Pen Cipher during the Christian Crusades."

Pig-Pen Cipher, is he fuckin' kidding me?

"All you need, Laddie Boy, is the example key to show you how each letter gets assigned to the grid."

Like I could understand that? Give me a freakin' abacus and let me count the colored beads, then I'm good.

He began feverishly drawing on a yellow legal pad, his body hunched over, hiding his efforts from view. His upper body started shaking. First, it shook sideways. Then up and down, up and down. It was as if a puppeteer pulled his strings and was controlling his vertebrae.

"Madame Evangeline, I got ya now—FuckYeahFuckYeahFuck-Yeah!"

Well, I can't tell you how happy I was to see my pal, Gerry, infected with a clear case of I'mSoFuckedINeedMyMedsToSeeMeStraight. Let's face it, my FineFeatheryFriends, as everyone knows, crazy needs company.

"OkayOkayOkayIGotIt!" The words exploded out of Gerry's puppet mouth as if riding on an exhalation of helium.

Holy shit, there is a God, I said to my brain, or was it the other way around?

He waved the letter in front of the screen. "The 29th, Boyo! The 29th!"

"The 29th?"

"If you miss the 19th, she'll be back again on the 29th!"

I pulled up my calendar. "That's two days from now!"

"Better call Maggie, Laddie Boy! Better call MaggieMaggie-DoggieDoggieChickieChickie!"

RSVP

In the end, I had to confess all. Maggie wasn't having my first, second, or third explanation. No, she wasn't having any of it.

"I'll see what I can do, but I can't promise anything."

We were FaceTiming and not the best way to make my case, but she was too busy to meet in person, so this would have to do.

"She knew my name? That blows my mind."

I caught Maggie in between showing apartments, and for the next fifteen minutes, she'd be alone in a penthouse apartment that had a gorgeous view of the Hudson River.

"How do you think I feel? She was my boss for five years." I surprised myself by talking in whole sentences. Perhaps my grip on sanity was holding.

"And, you're sure she's dead?" Mag's immediately realized her insensitivity and put her hand over her mouth in the act of contrition. "Oh Bernie, I didn't mean that!"

"Look, this is very weird," I said, trying to ease her embarrassment. I was sitting on a bench on one of the paths surrounding the oval in Stuyvesant Town. I was outside because I wasn't sure if I stayed in my apartment I could hold it together. I figured I couldn't wig out outdoors because security would see me, and the last thing I wanted was to give management a reason to kick me out of my rent-stabilized apartment. Ironically, at that very moment, I was totally alone. On the bright side, being alone allowed me to remove my mask; otherwise, my speech would be MaskMuddled and clear conversation would be fucked.

"But I'm the one who believes in Reincarnates." She was standing in front of a floor-to-ceiling window with the Hudson and Jersey waterfront in the background.

I nodded. "And ghosts, you believe in them, too, right?"

"Absolutely! You know, Bernie, it's no surprise that Madame Evangeline is contacting you. It's all part of the picture the Universe paints for us." She looked up at the sky, clear blue and so calm as if looking for confirmation that the Universe was indeed painting a picture of our future.

It's tempting to do the same, but the sudden stabbing pain in the pit of my stomach told me I wasn't ready to see my future, No-Siree-Bobcats, so I just nodded.

"Bernie, can you read to me exactly what she said?"

"I'm outside. I left the letter in the house."

That was a lie. I had the letter safely tucked away in the right front pocket of my recently re-ordered Levi's Men's 502 Original Fit, Dark Stonewash jeans.

"Do you think I can meet her?"

Boy, she has balls, I thought.

"Do you think Madame Evangeline would mind, Bernie?"

Now I'm thinking, sure, someone to lean on so I don't fuckin' fall on my face when the air turns freezing cold and out of the mist appears— what? I'll tell you what! Whatever it is scared the shit out of Bob Hope in The Ghost Breakers and made Abbot and Costello run like hell in Hold That Ghost, and that my FineFeatheryFriends, was good enough for me!

"I guess it's up to her," I said finally.

She smiled. "Bernie, do you still want me to ask someone for your friend?"

An older couple, the woman pushing a walker, the man shuffling alongside, holding her arm, was approaching. Both wore masks. I quickly fished mine out from my Eddie Bauer parka and immedi-

143

ately felt my hot breath back up into my face. I would have smothered if not for the man's sudden tirade, distracting me enough to change focus.

"How many times did I tell you, buy the one percent, buy the one percent," he screamed.

The woman paid no attention and kept pushing the walker.

"I know you're trying to kill me!" He clutched his heart with his free hand. "And don't think I'm not going to tell Dr. Polizzi when I see her!"

The woman kept pushing the walker and did not react as if she were deaf, as the man shouted in her ear.

Pointing to me, the man screamed, "He's my witness! I'm going to bring him to see Dr. Polizzi!"

The woman, never breaking stride, turned to me and pointed her finger at her head, and mouthed the words, "He's fucking nuts!"

"What's going on, Bernie? You okay?"

I had inadvertently pointed my iPhone toward the ground; however, Maggie could still hear the commotion. I pointed it back up to my face.

"Nothing. Just a domestic dispute."

"Bernie, I can't hear you with your mask on."

"Oh damn, sorry." I removed my mask, happy to see the couple had moved down the path and again deserted the area.

"So, should I get your friend a date? My friend Keri is always rendezvousing in empty apartments, sometimes for entire weekends."

"She never gets caught?"

"Oh, there have been times another broker set up a showing, and there came the unexpected knock at the door. One time, out in the Hamptons, Keri opens the door for a showing, puts the key back in the lockbox, and the next morning in walks another broker with her clients. Thank God it was the broker who caught her in the shower. And thank God the guy had already left."

"Word didn't get back to your boss?"

"Hell no. The other broker probably has done it too."

"How could she show the bathroom?"

"It was the Hamptons, babe. You could keep a family of four in those mansions and never run into the kids all season. Besides, at that level, the clients do a quick run-through, really only want to see the entertainment center, gym, pool, and the garage."

"The garage?"

"Climate control and four-post lifts are a must. Got to make it comfy cozy for the two Ferraris, Bentley, and the Range Rover."

I was embarrassed to ask, but I went for it anyway. "I think Gerry might want a picture."

"Tell him to go to our website, TheBayswaterAgency.com and check out Keri Rittenhouse under New York City representatives.

She saw me smiling and said, "Magnolia Swann, with two N's."

Hah! All this time, I thought Maggie stood for Margaret. Then it came to me. "Magnolia? Jesus, you're not..."

"From South Carolina?" She threw me a playful smile. "Next state over—Brevard, North Carolina. Born a Southern girl, just like Madame Evangeline."

I had nothing.

She tossed me another mischievous smile and said, "That's another reason I want to meet Madame Evangeline. I think we have a lot in common. Don't you, Bernie?"

I'm looking at her as if seeing her for the first time and thinking— no—not playful or mischievous, but wicked. Yes-Siree-Bobcats, this Maggie, aka Magnolia, was definitely one WickedlyWonderfulWoman.

YELLOW FLAGS
AND GREEN LIGHTS

Maggie and I agreed, so when I laid it out there were no slip-ups when I spoke to Gerry.

"OKAY, I got it, Laddie Boy. But you know, the ManlyGolden-ManRoot never leaves a job undone."

We were FaceTiming, so Gerry pushed his face closer to the screen and made sure I understood when he said, "The only time the ManlyGoldenManRoot doesn't finish what he starts is when he hears the sound of some yahoo comin' home when he ain't supposed to."

Suddenly, I had the image of Madame Evangeline's ghostly apparition floating into the room when Gerry and his ManlyGold-enManRoot are going to town and placing an icy ghoulish finger upon his bare backside and whispering, "Keri's husband is at the front door."

"Did I say somethin' funny, Laddie Boy?"

"Huh?"

"You're smilin', Boyo. What's so fuckin' funny?"

I came out of my reverie feet first and said, "Just imagining you going through the open window in just your tighty-whities."

He broke out into a grin. I was amazed at how quickly the lies were coming and how good they were.

"Not to worry, Laddie Boy. Got it down to a science."

"From what Maggie says, Keri won't be a problem. Not the curious type."

"Well, that's OKAY with me, but I would like to see this Madame Evangeline."

"I thought you didn't believe in ghosts? What changed your mind?"

"The letter, Boyo, the letter."

"The letter?" I was confused.

"TheCodeTheCode! ShitayToThePussay! I'm tellin' you; those Knights Templar were the first superheroes, seers who could look into the future and unlock its secrets. I bet they're still here, Laddie Boy. They're the secret hand behind Marvel Comics. Writin' TV shows like *The Twilight Zone*, *The X-Files*. All those stories are true, my man—and the Knights Templar are the storytellers!"

He knew I was thinking of my look-a-like, my doppelgänger, and wondering if I was a Knights Templar.

"You know, you really don't look like 'em. Besides, Duchovny's only an actor, a tool used by the Knights."

"I know," I said, not wanting to argue, tell him the truth about the power of the Hanky-Panky Man.

"So, how you wanna play it, Laddie Boy? Want me to go into the bathroom with you?"

"I was thinking of bringing Maggie."

"Shamhat? Is that what she's calling herself now? One of the holy harlots consecrated to the worship of the moon, ready to be ravished by the high priest with the Sky Bolt of Niurtra? That would be you—right, Boyo?"

"Shit, Gerry—you remembered."

"I remember everythin', Boyo, and the crazier, the more it gets imprinted up here." He pressed a finger against his forehead.

"She's no longer Shamhat. That was only when we were looking at the moon."

"Too bad. Sounds like you could use a holy harlot when you come face to face with a ghost. So, who is Shamhat now?"

I shrugged.

"You know her real name is Magnolia? I saw it on the website," he said, smiling as if revealing a secret truth.

I nodded.

"That's a Southern name."

I nodded again.

"Evangeline's a Southern name."

"I know." And I knew Gerry's mind was going where I had gone before.

"Boyo, there are no coincidences, only the illusion of coincidence." He gave me the famous and frequent GrinAndGlimmer-Stare. You know, the stare that says, GoOnBoyoTellMeTheNameOf-TheFilm?"

I made a V with the pointer and middle fingers and shoved it right up to the screen.

"*V for Vendetta.* Very fuckin' good, Laddie Boy! Very fuckin' good indeed!"

"Thanks." *It just so happened; I watched it the other day to see how heroes could comfortably wear masks.*

"So, you think because she's from the South, she's got an in with Madame Evangeline—that relationship's gonna protect you? Southern Ladies of The Confederacy, you know, like the Daughters Of The American Revolution—like that?"

"Maybe, maybe," *I repeated two more times in my head, each with more conviction.*

"Birds of a feather and shit like that, huh, Laddie Boy? Think this through, Boyo, and proceed with caution. Indie Rules. Yellow flags all the way, right, Laddie Boy?"

"The only way."

I Loved it when he went RaceCarLingo on me—knew he'd follow-up with something from Gran Prix. I was way ahead of him.

"The time for losing comes to every man, of course. I had not expected yours to come so soon," I said, giving him the full GrinAnd-GlimmerStare.

"Bernie, you fuck! That's one of my fav *Gran Prix* lines—Celi to Montand! When Montand's bitchin' about the car's performance."

"Ger, you deciphered it, right?"

"Right."

"Was there anything in it—a word—a hint on if I should come alone? Or maybe who I should bring?"

"No. I was just thinkin' if you needed help..."

"I just decided. I'm going in alone."

I could see he was thinking of another Gran Prix quote to throw back at me, so I thought it was time to change the subject.

"So, what did you think of Keri's photo? You think you two might hit it off?"

He came back to earth with a smile that flashed, GreenLightAll-TheWay. "A real CupCakeCutie."

"I bet she's better-looking in the flesh—Maggie was."

He nods.

"A BoDerekTen, Ger—a certifiable BoDerekTen," I say, loud and proud.

He's still nodding and asks, "And you sure she's a Dirty Girl, Boyo?"

"Ger, the only thing you should worry about is if you can keep up with her." I kept the smile to myself.

He grimaced. "The ManlyGoldenManRoot never disappoints, never ever—you should know that, Laddie Boy."

Ger threw me a FaceTimeFistBumpFuckYeahAirSalute, and while I joined him, I kept thinking, how do I keep my shit together when I'm meeting a ghost?

GHOST TIME

OkayOkayOkay! I'm one of those ChildrenOfTheSixO'Clock-Movie who thinks life mirrors the movies and not the other way round. While religion, school, the arts and science, show others the way, for moi, the truth comes at twenty-four frames per second, preferably in old-school black and white celluloid. That's my mantra, my motto, guide, and gospel.

Unfortunately, I'm weak, and it's hard to follow my faith; still, I'd like to believe that when I enter the guest bathroom at precisely 8 p.m., I will call upon every fiber in my celluloid and be TheSilverScreenHeroOfMyOwnMovie.

The first thing I do is become Roy Scheider in *All That Jazz*, but with one exception. Instead of splashing water on my face and looking into the mirror and yelling, "It's Showtime!" I improvise and scream, "It's Ghost Time!"

"That was very nice, Bernie," said a full-throated sultry, and beguiling female voice.

A sudden burst of intense, white light reflects off the mirror and forces me to shield my eyes.

"You're looking well," she continues; only this time softer, almost lyrically.

I turn, slowly open my eyes, and peak through splayed fingers, and watch a figure in a shimmering white dress gradually take shape and come to life.

Holy shit, it's Angelique, aka Jessica Lange!

"Come closer, Bernie."

Can a voice actually smile? I want to do as it says, but I can't seem to move.

"You needn't be afraid, Bernie. You read my letter."

Sure, why the fuck not? I'm already a Three on the NuttyAsAFruitCakeScale; why not go all the way to a Ten?

"That's it; just a few steps closer."

I'm pissed I didn't think to wear a wire; that way, the others could hear what's going on and get the fuck in here and give me some backup.

"Give me your hand," she said sweetly.

"But that'll leave me with only one." That's a line from Arthur, and I want to say it, but a little voice in my head warns me this is not the time for being a wiseass.

"Bernie, open and close your eyes three times. Do it slowly; take your time," said the apparition.

I do as I'm told, and I see that the figure slowly transforms from Angelique, aka Jessica Lange, into Madame Evangeline Morris.

"Now isn't that better," said the apparition.

She's looking more like herself every second. I nod and can smile again. Praise God that rigor mortis has lessened its hold on me and I can actually move my lips and smile.

"Bernie, didn't I write in the letter that you have the strength and courage to carry out my instructions?"

Rule numbers One, Two, and Three: Never argue with a dead person who can talk and shape-change simultaneously.

"I knew from reading your chart that you would use your MoviesAsLifeFixation to give you strength and courage. When you did your Joe Gideon shtick, I naturally assumed that if I materialized as Angelique, that would seamlessly feed into that idée fixe and make my entrance less frightening."

How fucked is that? However, rules four to ten say, "keep to one nod and one smile, and do not fall to your knees and kiss the feet of a ghost thinking that will save your ass."

I nod and praise God. I thank Him for helping me form a convincing smile.

"Bernie, for the next week, as proscribed by The Opening, I am permitted to act as your guide. I am also allowed to materialize as any movie character, male or female, if that is your choice."

I continued to follow the rules One to Three. I'm also keeping my mouth shut because, shit—to see a ghost, that may be a' three' on the Nutty-AsAFruitCakeScale, but to carry on a conversation with one, that is definitely a ten!

"Bernie, I was serious when I told you not to be sad, for I am leaving the Planet of The Sorrowful Star for the celestial glory of eternal life."

Her smile warmed my face, and I think this is all a hallucination because I got the Covid, and I'm in the ICU, on a ventilator, and ThisIs-TheEndMyFriend.

"Bernie, you can talk to me. I won't bite."

"What happens after a month?" *Oh fuck, you dumbass! Number 10 to 20; don't ask any questions you don't already know the answers to!*

"You will no longer require guidance."

"Why me?" *Fuck the rules! I need answers.* Why can I talk to furniture, speak to you—a..."

"Dead person. Go on, you can say it."

"You are dead, right?"

"In your world, that would be correct."

OkayOkayOkayOnwardAndSideways. "But why me?"

"Bernie, it is your destiny."

Oh, there it was again, like in her letter, 'the destiny thing'. "You read it in my palm the first time we met?"

"Yes."

"And then you did my astrological chart. What—to make sure you hadn't read me wrong?"

"It was the follow-up, Bernie. Part of the grand plan set forth by The Opening."

Ah, shit, here it is again, The Opening. I'm getting a bad vibe. Starting to feel the opening is like a never-ending dark pit that will swallow me whole.

I must have looked like death warmed over; now that's ironic when I'm talking to a ghost. Nevertheless, Madame Evangeline thought it best to give me a reassuring smile, and I threw one back and said, "But you never told me. You went on as if everything was normal. You hired me. We worked together for eleven years."

"It was not meant to be."

"You knew everything about me. That I was..."

"Sweet on me? Yes."

"You never..."

"Showed you any encouragement. Again, not meant to be."

"Talking to furniture was meant to be? Having a Reincarnate—Mary Shelley—to have her take over my body—that was meant to be?"

"No—that is your choice."

Tell me, who in their right state of mind could process such a bizarre idea, let alone someone like me, an admixture of Pussyhound, Wonder Boy, and FraidyCatPussyWussySnowFlakeRentBoy whose motto is, 'Be afraid, be very afraid'.

"Bernie, as your guide, I am permitted to assist you as long as we stay within the parameters set forth by The Opening."

For a moment, I forgot I was looking at and talking to a dead woman. Not any mortal woman, but a woman who I had worked closely with, eight hours a day, for almost eleven years. A woman, I had a yen for those eleven years. Fortunately, I had brought with me a paper clip (ala Harry Palmer) that I dug into the palm of my hand, creating just enough pain to get me back on track (ala Ipcress File) and think. Opening? Maybe not a never-ending dark pit but perhaps like an opening act? As in some cosmic comic, warming up the crowd for whom, the fucking Romulans?

So I ask, "The Opening?

"The Opening, Bernie...is that from where all matter originates and flows."

Fuck me! I should have guessed—The Ghost and Ghoul Highway! I dug the clip deeper into my palm; otherwise, I'd be singing Highway To Hell in my head.

"Bernie, is there anything else you wish to ask me?"

I'm having one of my IHaveNothingMoments.

"Questions you might have?"

"Questions," I whisper. "Questions? We don't need no stinkin' questions." *I'm so fucked! I'm fucking with lines from The Treasure Of The Sierra Madre.*

"Questions regarding your Reincarnate, Mary Shelley. For example, do you wish for her to enter your consciousness?"

"And do what, turn me into a woman?" *That just came out, without thinking but who the fuck cares, right?*

"Bernie, are you asking me if your Reincarnate can change your sex?"

In for a penny, in for a pound, when you go down the rabbit hole, but I'm not totally a moron, so I say UngotzungoolBupkisNoneNadaZip.

"Then Bernie, the answer is, she will take control of your mind and body, and if your Reincarnate so wishes, she can change your hormonal composition, and yes, she can change you into a woman."

I gave her my best AhSoGrasshopperSmile. I'm now so out of fucking control I'm doing looks from Kung Fu.

"Bernie," she continued, "it is in your destiny to make that choice."

Get a girlish figure and lose your dick! Good luck with that. Rule number one hundred... 'One can never be so fucked that you lose your sense of humor'.

WE ARE GATHERED
HERE TODAY

"Lemme see your hand."

"Here." I stretched out my left hand to show Gerry the bandage covering the self-inflicted wound in my palm.

"She did that?" said Keri, whose voice echoed from inside a wine goblet half-filled with Chardonnay.

Gerry and I shared an imperious glint of superiority and then gazed at her with the stare that said, DummyHaven'tYouEverSeen-TheIpcressFiles?

"I did it to myself, and Madame Evangeline bandaged me up." *I thought it was time to get Keri's head out of the wine glass, so I asked,* "Could you top me off, Keri?"

Gerry mouthed the words; *I really like her*, and then gave me a WinkADink, then eyed Keri with the look of a shark circling prey.

Maggie held up her empty wine glass, and Keri got the message and yanked a bottle from the gold ice bucket, saw it was empty and deftly pulled out another. "Time to open number three!"

The ice bucket was at my knee, and I plucked out one of the empty bottles and glanced at the label again. It was a 1985 Potel, Maison Nicolas Puligny Montrachet les Combettes, one of three Maggie pulled out of the largest floor-to-ceiling wine cabinet I had ever seen. Actually, it wasn't a cabinet, but an entire temperature-controlled room that she had led me to, without the aid of a map or GPS. She had grabbed three bottles of white, and seeing my bandaged hand, gave me one and kept two for herself, explaining that we could always come back for more.

"Last bottle, huh? Okay—Ker—you take care of the boys, and I'll go for more supplies." She got up to leave. "Hey, Ker, why don't you show the boys your cork trick?" said Maggie.

"What cork trick?" asked Gerry.

Keri giggled. "I used to tend bar, sweetie. Held the record at every place I worked, including some gigs at private parties where the guests would take bets on how fast I could open a bottle, spit the cork in the air and catch it, all with my eyes blindfolded."

"Like assembling a rifle in the dark, huh?" said Gerry.

"Absolutely!" giggled Keri. Then Keri closed her eyes and began unscrewing the cork by holding it in her mouth while she worked the corkscrew with her right hand. When she finished, still with her eyes closed, she spat the cork up in the air and caught it as it dropped down. The catch reminded me of the 'Say Hey Kid', Willie Mays, who made the basket-catch famous.

Gerry and I broke out in applause.

Keri opened her eyes and gave us a half-bow. Then she looked over at me and said, "Bernie, I don't know what you have, but I've never seen Maggie so happy."

Before I could reply, Keri was up, filling my glass and smiling into my face, not that I had anything to say. "You're not hung like a Rhino, are you Bernie?"

That got Gerry to move faster than I had ever seen and, with an empty goblet in his outstretched hands, bellowed, "That would be me, BabyCakes, and as soon as you refill me, I will CrossYourEyes-AndDotYourSweetSpot as only the ManlyGoldenManRoot can."

Suppose I hadn't illegally entered a multimillion apartment to have a conversation with the ghost of a dead woman I'd had a crush on for eleven years? And suppose I hadn't stolen three bottles of 1985 Potel, Maison Nicolas Puligny Montrachet les Combettes, to celebrate my encounter? In that case, I might have argued with Gerry as to who had the bigger Johnson.

But what ReallyReallyTrulyTrulySeriouslyFolks got me off my game was the chuckle coming from behind Gerry and Keri. The laugh, only I heard, from the woman, only I could see. We'd never come close to having even a kiss, SoSoSo you can BetYourBottomBippy Madame Evangeline had never seen me in my birthday suit— SoSoSo–how could she be so freakin' sure I'm not hung like a Rhino? HuhHuhHuh!

"More vino!" shouted Maggie, who was rolling three wine bottles toward us over the oval medallion that stood out against the ornate floral design of the antique French Aubusson rug...a rug I knew to be museum quality and not a reproduction.

I quickly scooped up the bottles before they bumped into each other, risked cracking open, and gently placed each into the ice bucket.

Turning, Maggie said, "Back with more goodies in a sec," and then she was gone.

"Bernie, I'm glad you were paying attention when we went to examine the carpets and rugs at the Met," said Madame Evangeline, who had taken my seat when I went to pick up the rolling bottles.

I looked over to Gerry and Keri to see if they were as surprised as I was to see Madame Evangeline, but they appeared lost in their own world, eyeballing each other like dogs in heat.

"Don't worry, Bernie. They can't see us."

"Like in *The Ghost and Mrs. Muir*?"

"I always preferred *Blithe Spirit*. I can make myself look like Elvira—Kay Hammond—if you like," said Madame Evangeline.

"You're more the Constance Cumming's type."

"I can do her," said Madame Evangeline. Want to see?"

"No! Stop!"

"Bernie, don't get excited. Come sit. I can stand."

In a flash, Madame Evangeline was up, and I was sitting in the chair.

"How the...?"

"Bernie, please, no profanity. You were so good in my shop, but as soon as you and Gerry get together, you're like two school children who can't wait to get into the playground so you can shout every dirty word you just learned."

Looking around, I could see Gerry and Keri frozen in place, and I got the message, loud and clear. I was in RealTwighlightZoneShit and had no choice but to GoAlongToGetAlongHopalongCassidy.

"Bernie, did you know the title Blithe Spirit was devised out of the poem "To a Skylark" written by Percy Bysshe Shelley, who happens to be the husband of..."

"Mary Shelley, the Reincarnate that wants my body—I know—I know."

Madame Evangeline nodded, then gazed over at Gerry and Keri. "Bernie, if it bothers you to see your friends in suspended animation, I can do this."

And in a blink of an eye, Gerry and Keri came alive and continued their StuckLikeGlueBecauseI'mStuckOnYouEyeballing as if never uninterrupted.

"How?"

"It's called Dimensional Paralleling. It can be accessed and sustained for short periods, but Bernie, if it makes you more comfortable, I'm able to maintain it for the length of my stay here."

What's the saying; choose between the devil and the deep blue sea?

I glanced over at Gerry and Keri, then back at Madame Evangeline. "Whatever," I said, figuring I'd solve the problem by pretending we were the only two people in the room.

"Bernie, have you come to a decision?"

"About what?"

Madame Evangeline smiled. "Asking me another question."

"Why have you never come back to New York since you closed the shop? You have never kept in touch, either. I thought we were..."

"Friends? We are friends, Bernie, and I apologize, but I had my reasons. Unfortunately, one of the negative consequences of my decision meant ending our relationship, for which I am truly sorry."

Madame Evangeline—apparition, spirit, ghost, or simply parlor trickster, was—by my side and extending her right hand. My fingers were white-knuckling the arms of the chair in the reverse neck choke, aka shime-waza (if I tell you more, I'd have to kill you). But Madame Evangeline, WhamBangShazamed my right mitt and had it flying up to take hers in the most appropriate of appropriately Gentlemanly-GentleGripsARoony.

Her touch lit up my prefrontal cortex, and my high-level thinking neurons kicked in, sending the message to the rest of my body that I had a functioning head on my shoulders capable of machine-gunning out a barrage of relatively sane questions.

"Will I think like her—feel like her—remember me—just disappear—become a woman—will...?"

She squeezed my hand, and the neurons ceased firing, and I became silent.

"Bernie, think of your Reincarnate as a single idea that generates thoughts and emotions, setting off a new pattern of behavior. If you dismiss it out of hand, your demeanor will remain the same. Perhaps, you become so enamored and enthralled with your new emotions that you will happily change your conduct? Or, will these new thoughts provoke fear and anger and mistrust...even devolve into obsessive behavior? Will you fight it, Bernie? Will you defend yourself at all costs until you banish the Reincarnate from your mind and body?"

How the fuck do I know? Hold on, GhostWoman! I reached for her hand. "Truth or dare?"

I'm a little fuzzy on whether she would answer because Maggie had returned and was talking, no screaming—OkayOkayOkay, maybe not screaming in my ear, "Bernie, Bernie, who are you talking to?"

CAN I HAVE A
SNICKERS BAR?

"It's not that I doubt you, but Bernie, you have to admit, it is a little strange that you were the only one to see her, even though you say she was in the living room with us all the time."

OkayOkayOkay, this was not what I had in mind as we sat close to each other on the bed, in what I guessed was the master bedroom. A smile, a romantic word or two, accompanied by a caress; whatever the little head uses to control the big head under HotToTrotConditions.

"I know that's the way it is in the movies, Bernie. What's that one with Rex Harrison?"

"Blithe Spirit," I said.

"Yes, that's the one! But, Bernie, this is real life. And don't forget, if anyone has an affinity for ghosts, it's me. Remember, I see my Reincarnate in conversations with other people. You do see my point, don't you, Bernie? You can understand why it is hard for me to believe that a ghost appeared to only you and not to me?"

I was amazed and a little frightened at how lucid Maggie appeared, considering at the very least, she consumed an entire bottle of the 1985 Potel, Maison Nicolas Puligny Montrachet les Combettes on her own. I performed my SherlockHomesScanARooney. No swaying, slumping, slurring, unfocused eyes, or signs of faulty memory. In her state of clarity, she would perform an interrogation with focus and precision, and unless I could come up with a satisfying explanation, forget any chance of hanky-panky, now or in the future.

"Bernie, I understand she might not have wanted me in the bathroom. But what about when we were all in the living room? She might have at least thanked me for bandaging your hand."

"I'm sure it wasn't personal. You've more contact with your Reincarnates and with the spirit world than I have. I mean, your Ms. Murat writes fairy tales and ghost stories. What about your Casper The Friendly Ghost dreams?"

How's that for quick thinking? Shit, I'm on a roll!

"You're right," she agreed.

"Kindred souls, right?"

I was going to add birds of a feather, but less is more, right?

Maggie nodded. "But Bernie?"

"Yes, Maggie?"

"Why didn't she come out and talk to me?"

Suddenly the lyrics to Micky and Silvia's song, "Love is Strange," popped into my head.

"Unless..." she said.

I almost said "yes, *Silvia*," but instead said, "yes, Maggie."

"It was all in your head."

Now that pronouncement, my FineFeatheryFriends, is a showstopper and a head-scratcher.

"Ever think it's all up there," she said, pointing to my head.

What a place to be! Naturally, I kept that wisecrack to myself; but shit, suppose that was the truth of it? What if I'm a delusional headcase? Nah! My little head would never buy it. You can take the boy out of wonder, but you can't take the wonder out of the boy once the meds go down the gullet!

"Bernie, if we can't be totally honest with each other, I'm going to have to reconsider our relationship."

Again, I had nothing, and Maggie wasn't going to wait until I did. She got up and walked to the door...a door I noticed for the first time was covered in white fur. I looked around. Fuck me! So are the walls! Fuck me twice more—the ceilings are mirrored!

"Just noticing it now, Bernie?" And with that, she was out the door.

The Uber driver adjusted his rearview to get his rocks off as Gerry was going down on Keri. I powered down my window, telescoped my head out, closed my eyes, and gulped as much cold fresh air into my lungs as I could without choking.

I opened my eyes, and Tourneau's Time Machine window, with its array of glowing white clocks displaying various world city times, blinded me for an instant.

I blinked, and there I was, standing on the sidewalk, watching me staring at me through the open car window until the Uber crossed Madison Avenue and was gone.

"Bernie, I know how much you liked *The Big Clock,* so I thought Tourneau's Time Machine window would be appropriate."

Madame Evangeline's Ghost was at my side (but of course she was), so I casually replied, "Gruesome ending."

"As bad as *The Stranger?*"

"Falling down an elevator shaft or having a moving clock tower figure impale you with a sword? Pick your poison," I replied.

Dear Abby, I'm playing movie trivia with DeadWomanWalking! Can you help? Yours truly, Bernie In Delirium.

"Bernie, don't forget Harold Lloyd hanging on by his fingernails to the hands of a huge detached clock face while dangling high above street level while down below, traffic is speeding by," continued a smiling and full-bodied, Madame Evangeline.

Dear Bernie In Delirium, Go with the flow and remember, nobody's perfect. Yours truly, Dear Abby.

So I went with it!

"*Safety First,*" I said, addressing the apparition. "The movie's called *Safety First!*"

"*Safety First!* How ironic, don't you think so, Bernie?"

"So, who's in the Uber?"

"Why you, of course, Bernie."

Ordinarily, it would have taken me a lifetime of taking it lying down (a ShrinkTalkingShitAboutMyMother), but NoTimeForFig-uringOutDeepDoDoWhenYourTalkingToAGhost, so I FiredUp-NeuronCentral and say "A doppelgänger!"

"Bernie, that's not exactly what we call it, but the concept's the same."

"And you can just pluck me out of any scene while you leave my double carrying on as if nothing's wrong?"

"If you mean will he be able to tip the Uber driver and find his way up to your apartment—not to worry, Bernie, you will be back in time for that."

"I'm glad. Don't want my twin going overboard with the tip or stiffing the driver and getting me blackballed from Uber and every other ride-sharing app."

When Madame Evangeline gave me a MommyComforting-HerBabyShoulderHug, I remembered how! "Dimensional Parallel-ing. Isn't that what you called it?"

"Yes, Bernie. That is exactly how."

OkayOkayOkay, I admit when I first heard the term, it was as opaque as deciphering *Dune*; however, now it came to me. Dimensional Paralleling was the ethereal equivalent to parallel parking, to which I excelled. I was about to prove my genius when she put her hand to my mouth and whispered, "Be silent. Don't speak—no, don't speak. Silence."

FuckMeSideWaysToTheCemeteryOnSunday, Madame Evangeline had just turned into Dianne Wiest and was doing lines from 'Bullets Over Broadway'!

The thundering air horn from Rescue One made me jump, and WhamBamShazamMa'am, Actress Dianne was gone, and Madame Evangeline was gently rubbing my shoulder and reassuring me with her spectral smile.

I wondered if all ghosts had this ability, or did it have to be your Reincarnate? HoldTheFuckingPhoneSeniorWettingHisPantsNow, Madame Evangeline can't be your Reincarnate; she's not in your gene pool, or is she?

"Walk with me, Bernie," said the ghost.

Had Madame Evangeline done the Maggie impersonation of Marty Feldman and said, "Walk this way," I would have thrown in the towel and said, fuck it—let the monsters loose and turn me into Mary Shelley. But Madame Evangeline didn't do any Young Frankenstein, so I played it like it laid and put one foot in front of the other and accompanied her across 57th Street and into the lobby of the Four Seasons hotel.

The masked-up doorman opened the outer door with a welcoming nod, and I realized Madame Evangeline had slapped a mask on me, so I entered without a problem. As to Madame Evangeline, I could feel her hand but had no idea whether we appeared as an arm and arm CoupleCouple, or I was a single plus OnePhantom. My heart was racing, but you can BetYourSweetBippyBoysAndGirls, this FraidyCatPussyWussySnowFlakeRentBoy whose motto is, 'be afraid, be very afraid' —would keep eyes StraightOnLaserFocusedMouth-ShutTighterThanBarkOnATree, UntilUntil...yeah...UntilUntilUntil what?

TRAVELIN' THRU

It was the following morning, and we were FaceTiming. Gerry's hunched over and barely able to speak.

"You okay? What's the matter?"

Gerry lifted his head inches from the tabletop and looked at me the way a wrestler looks at the ref after being body slammed to the canvas. He groped for an open plastic container, coaxed a couple of pills into his mouth, and with his other hand managed to lift a container of Ocean Spray Cran-Pomegranate halfway to his mouth before the pain was so great he had to put it down and swallow the pills dry.

"Do you want me to call your doctor? Come over?"

"I think I'm in love."

"I could hop in a cab and be there in twenty minutes."

"Keri's gone out for a heating pad, and I've got plenty of Vicodins."

"I thought you had a heating pad?"

"She's getting me one with the moist heat. Says it's the best." He lifted his

head. "Did you hear me? I said I'm in love?"

"That's nice."

He grimaced as he straightened up. "Don't be a prick, Bernie. Just because you don't have a BabyCake." He grimaced again. "Oh fuck, that hurts."

"Maybe you should call your doctor?"

"And say what? I was having sex on a fuckin' balance beam with a woman who thought she was Simone Biles?"

I thought about smiling; instead, I was distracted by a tug at my sleeve. "Be silent. Don't speak—no, don't speak. Silence." *Fuck me; was that coming from my lips?*

Gerry's mouth opened in amazement and murmured, "You know, when you do Dianne Wiest, you look like her. Anyone ever tell you that, Boyo?"

"Yeah, the first time I threw you a *Bullets Over Broadway* line."

"Hey Laddie Boy, I'm sorry I said that shit about you being jealous. It's the drugs, talkin'."

"Love means never having to say you're sorry." Oh, fuck, I didn't say that!

Madame Evangeline, her ghost, made me do it. I hate fucking *Love Story*!"

"Yeah, Laddie Boy, but it's still a fuckin' great line." Gerry did his best to refocus his eyes before he said, "She in the room, now, Boyo?"

I looked around. There was no one.

"Let me see her."

I didn't respond.

"She's not there, is she, Boyo?"

"No, I guess not."

"But she does movie lines?"

I nodded. "She does the lines to relax me."

"What the fuck!"

"When she first appeared in the bathroom, she looked like Jessica Lange in *All That Jazz.*"

"Figures."

"Huh?"

"You know what death with dignity is, man? You don't drool."

"I don't remember that line."

"Yeah—look it up. It's there. So, Laddie Boy, is she as good as me?"

"Huh?"

"Movie lines? Is she as good as me?"

When I didn't respond, he tossed me a look that said, JustPutYourHandInALightSocketAndWakeTheFuckUp, and said, "I know why you're not answerin' me, Boyo. I bet she only does lines from pictures about banshee shit. Am I right?"

One long hard tug, and then I heard me say, "People say nothing is impossible, but I do nothing every day."

Gerry looked stumped, then he threw down TheIDon'tBelieveThisShitStare and said, "She just gave you that one?"

I nodded. I nodded because there was no other way that line could have popped into my head.

"Can I talk to her? I mean, who the fuck am I talkin' to now? You or her?"

I looked down at my right sleeve and then up into the empty airspace. No SpookyShiveringMistyColdCemeteryOpenCoffinBansheeMusicGhoulsAndGhostShit. UngotzungoolBupkisNoneNadaZip.

"She can make people appear in two places at the same time," I said.

"You know, don't you, Bernie, that some people get all fucked up on meds—me, I'm the opposite. When I'm flying high, high above the shit, I can see things other people can't." He tossed me the stare that said, ICanSeeClearlyNowSoDon'tFuckWithMe, and continued. "Bernie, I believe you're like me. You're a highflyer."

I was a day late and a dollar short with my synaptic transmissions, and Gerry read my slowness as dullness, so he schooled me on his Highflyer theory.

"Bernie—me with my pain meds, you with your little blue pills, and whatever else you mix in. They open doors closed to others. You feel me, Laddie Boy?"

"Madame Evangeline said all life comes from The Opening."

"Didn't I just say that, Boyo! Madame Evangeline and I are on the same fuckin' wavelength, Laddie Boy—on the same f'in wavelength!"

Well, InTheTimeOfGhostsDoppelgängersAndHallucinations—good news is good news; so naturally, his words lifted my spirits and made my heart sing.

"Come to Papa, Laddie Boy. What else does Madame Evangeline do to relax your ass?"

"Oh no! That's really sick, even for you, Gerry."

"What—LickieSuckie with a ghost?"

"Gerry, can you hear yourself?"

"Laddie Boy, don't get your draws in an uproar. I mean, when you're JuicingTheJuiceman, what's the diff between rubbin' one off with GhostWoman, or SpillinTheSeedWithYourSilverScreenBabyCake?"

I got the picture. To Gerry, it was just another JackOffTotalReleaseOfTheJohnson.

"Why do you think we haven't gotten the Covid, Boyo?"

"Huh?"

I'm in total SynapticShutDown and remain frozen in time, or is it my Doppelgänger sitting here, and I'm on a beach, in Hawaii, sipping pina Coladas and having my back rubbed by the mind-blowingly beautiful Jessica Lange?

"Bernie, I'm talkin' to you. I'm askin' you. Why the fuck do you think we haven't gotten sick?"

I have to leave Hawaii; that much I know. I blink twice, get my bearings. Lucille, fuckin' Lucille! Didn't I have this conversation with Lucille? I know the fuckin' answer! I know it!

"My Reincarnate," I shout. "MaryFuckin'Shelley!"

"Not exactly..."

OhOhOh, I got it, I got it, I got it!

"The Universe! The Universe!"

"Not exactly..."

*OkayOkayOkay, everybody comes to the end of their rope, n'est pas?
So I give 'em both barrels.* "If you let my mind go now, that'll be the end of it. I will not look for you. I will not pursue you. But if you don't, I will look for you, I will find you, and I will kill you."

"Fuckin'LiamTakeNoPrisonersNeeson!" I like that, Bernie. No, I love that!"

We did our FaceTimeFistBumpFuckYeahAirSalute.

"OkayOkayOkay, The reason you are immune to the Covid is your ability to change consciousness! It's mind over body, Bernie— mind over fuckin' body!"

Before I could react, Gerry grabbed a paperclip and moved it from one hand to another, and then he held out his fists. "Which one, Boyo?"

How the fuck should I know? I'd seen him do this shit a hundred times and never could I get it right.

"Which one, Boyo?"

Oh, please take me back to fuckin' Hawaii!

"Choose!"

I pointed. "Left!"

"You're pointing to my right hand?"

"Yeah...right."

He opened his right fist. It was empty. You could have driven a semi through the smile on his face.

"I'd do it again, but you'd be wrong, and you know why Boyo?"

I shook my head. At least, I think that was the part of my body that was moving. Unfortunately, I wasn't communicating with my frontal lobe and consequently feeling a bit adrift and unconnected so I wouldn't bet the farm.

"Because I distracted you, made you change consciousness, and that, Laddie Boy, can be a bad thing, but it can be a good thing."

Good news! My senses were returning! Bad news! I swear I smelled the smoke from my neurons that were now misfiring, and I definitely heard the crackling of the burning dendrites.

Gerry smiled. "You understand when I say—a good thing?"

No question, my brainpan was frying up, and it was only a question of time before smoke would be coming out of my ears.

"I know I've been pushin' the pus-say..."

"And Reincarnates! And the OpenSeamInTheUniverse."

"Patience, Grasshopper, patience."

"What, you deny it?"

"CollaterialConsciousChangingDistraction but..."

Fuck me. That sounded very cool, but I wasn't interrupting Gerry because he was on a roll.

"You, my friend, have discovered a more powerful distraction, ghosts! Even more, fuckin' fantastic, Laddie Boy, is how your SpiritChick turns into the HollywoodLadyDuJour, SlipSlidin'TheGoldenManroot into a CinematicClimax, the envy of every swingin' dick on Planet JLo. Laddie Boy, there are diversions, and there are diversions, but this SelfServeSilverScreenJamboree—man—you have shown me is one-hundred percent effective against the Covid— one-hundred percent effective! You got to bottle it, Boyo! Bottle it and drink from it, and no virus is EverEverEver gonna fuck with your PleasurePalaceOfDelusionAndDelirium. Can I have an amen!"

SLIPSTREAM OF LIFE

I t's been four months, and measure for measure, as the bard said, all is copasetic. The promise of a vaccine coming to an arm in your neighbor this fall has put everyone in a more positive frame of mind. I no longer think about signing up for any Covid trial, although Donna, with Meryl's help, is participating in one and hasn't contracted the virus so far.

Gerry's vertebrae are one hundred percent better, thanks to Keri, who has done a one-eighty. Instead of using his body as a balance beam, she had her Thai acupuncturist/masseuse provide 'jungle' treatments that have Gerry standing up straight as an I-Beam, something I haven't witnessed since he became addicted to jerking off.

I left BackAgain.com and the world of online dating and no longer yearned for what is DNAAndMe. My departure resulted in Dr. Keys reaching out to discover why I was no longer a member. There are emails, texts, phone calls, each more and more urgent. The big reveal came in the last phone call. Had I been acting differently, had there been a change in my personality? If so, had these changes coincided with a visit by a distant relative? Had I been diagnosed with Covid-19? These messages were code for, hey Bernie, sorry for opening up a seam in the Universe and letting your dead relatives jump out of the ancestral gene pool into your ependymal canal. In other words, Bernie Max, I let the dogs in!

I spend the majority of my HappyHappinessTime writing a children's book. It's about a little boy and a tree frog finding *their* HappyHappinessTime when they meet as ghosts and exchange identities. Although I feel the influence of Mary Shelley and hear her voice as I write (more on that later or not), the book is more a combination of *Tootsie, Scarface,* and *Brian's Song,* rather than *Frankenstein: or, The Modern Prometheus.*

The working title is *The Boy and The Tree Frog Go To Hell,* and already I see a market for kids who are into role-playing.

I have to confess my creative juices have never been more Juicy-JuicedUp. Scenarios, plot twists, and character developments continue igniting my dendrites, setting my neurons banging up against my cerebellum like caged birds trying to escape captivity! A children's book! Who would have thought?

I've held off long enough, and I think it's about time I address the GhostInTheRoom, or better still, the GhostThatIsn'tInTheRoom. Yes, my FineFeatheryFriends, Madame Evangeline's ghost (this one, or the one running in Dimension Parallel, or any other lane the doppelgänger lives), is UngotzungoolBupkisNothingNadaZip.

I do attempt to contact Madame Evangeline and ask her to get me back in the program. I tell her I'm having mental symptoms of DimensionParallelWithdrawal, DPW for short. I admit I might have been a little too casual, too blasé about being in a room when a Ghost, *you,* appear as a movie character to ease my anxiety. How about, how cool as the other side of a pillow, when *you* transport other people into another dimension so you and I can have a private tête a tête? OrOrOr, best of all, when you split me/you into two, and I get transporting off to wine and dine at The Four Seasons while my loser Doppelgänger has to listen to his Uber driver bitch about the traffic. GoddamnThatWasSomeSpecialShit.

OkayOkayOkay—maybe I need her help to deal with my Reincarnate. It's not like I'm addicted to Mary's energy. I can go an entire day without any new ideas. OkayOkayOkay—I haven't tried to because—like man–my entire body is ElectricCity! *The Boy and The Tree Frog Go To Hell* is just the beginning! It's like when they produced the first Superman or Spider-Man comic. You just knew there were tons more epic adventures to come. Can you feel me?

Thank God for Maggie. She has been my OneWomanSupportTeam, keeping me sane while I've been in DimensionParallelRecovery. This wonderful magical lady keeps the FlamesOfFantasyFucking burning hot and heavy. I don't believe we've stolen into the exact libidinous location twice, and I'm talking once a week TrystingTheNightAway for the last four months. That's how many FunHouseFuckPads? Sixteen—yep—sixteen MardiGrasOfTheFlesh, and there is no end in sight. The woman is a ConjurerOfCarnalCarnivorCelebrityReincarnates. One great movie title and reminiscent of *The Man With A Thousand Faces,* only with a lot more fucking.

By the way, remember how I had a little trouble with the GhostsInTheRoomWhileWeDoIt. Well, I've come to the grown-up decision, the dead deserve to get their rocks off too, so I don't care anymore who did what to whom in our PleasureDomesOfTheLickieSuckie.

Here's an interesting factoid: Miss Maggie can morph into six different Reincarnates and rotate them in and out; so I never know who will show up for our next MardiGrasOfTheFlesh. Another surprise, the moment she drops me at my front door, she becomes MaggieTrueSelf, CorrectoColonFullStopInTheNameOfLove. She kisses me GoodnightMoonBeamsForBernie, leaving me with the impression her Reincarnates go post tryst and do not ComeOutToPlayLet'sPretend, until our next assignation.

I mentioned her gifts to Gerry because Maggie's behavior adds some believability to Donna's belief in Reincarnates that left opened, no pun intended, to OpenSeamsInTheUniveriseTheory; further throwing shade, in my opinion, on Dr. Keys for causing this CelestialCalamity.

"Didn't I tell you, you got to bottle her, Boyo? Bottle her and drink from her, and no virus is EverEverEver gonna fuck with your PleasurePalaceOfDelusionAndDelirium!"

Gerry jumped to his feet. I jumped to my feet, and together, we did our FaceTimeFistBumpFuckYeahAirSalute.

Gerry wasn't done, not by a long shot. He pushed his face right up to the screen and said, "Your mission, Bernie Max, should you decide to accept it, is to call MaggieOfAThousandNewVaginas, and slip through the seams in the Universe on a stream of LoveJuice and never look back. As always, should you or any of *your* personalities be slow on the uptake and risk gettin' the Covid, or any other shit the world throws at you Boyo, I will disavow any knowledge of your FraidyCatPussyWussySnowFlakeRentBoyAss. This tape will self-destruct in five seconds. Good luck, Laddie Boy, should you decide to take on the mission."

And with that pretty decent impression of the never seen *Mission Impossible* controller, the voice on the tape which gave Dan Briggs and James Phelps their assignments, Gerry was standing now, his arms flailing, his oohing sounds chilling. Damn, all he needed was a bedsheet, and he could seriously pass for Casper The Ghost. Then—then—Gerry motioned me up again and began singing and gyrating.

Love
Love is strange
Lot of people
Take it for a game
Once you get it
You never want to quit, no no
After you've had it
You're in an awful fix

He reached out to me, beckoning me to join him.

Bernie
Yes, Gerry
How does your ManlyManRoot call your lover girl
Come here, lover girl
And if Maggie MaggieOfAThousandNewVaginas doesn't answer
Oh lover girl
And if Maggie MaggieOfAThousandNewVaginas still doesn't answer
I simply say
Baby, oh baby
My sweet baby, you're the one
Baby, oh baby
My sweet baby, you're the one.

After we did another FaceTimeFistBumpFuckYeahAirSalute and broke the connection, I sat down and took the opportunity to catch my breath. First, out of the corner of my left eye, and then the right, I spied a pair of gold-rimmed rearview mirrors. The coast was clear. It was time to switch lanes. Time to change consciousness. Time to slip through the SlipSeamOfLife.

THE END

ABOUT THE AUTHOR

Eric Robespierre was born and raised in New York City. He has worked as a screenwriter, playwright, documentary film director and web designer. He has been an award winning advertising copywriter creating campaigns for Mitsubishi, Izod Lacoste, and other major brands.

Robespierre is now a full-time writer. Together with Helen Brand he wrote *The Yummy Hunter's Guide: The Best-Tasting, Low-Calorie Foods and Where to Shop for Them*. He is also the author of *Cracking the Walnut: How Being a Little Nuts Helped Me to Beat Prostate Cancer*, *Living Large in America: The Life and Times of the Family Ginsburg (Pronounced Du Pont)*, *Lighten Up And Log In For Love: How Humor Helps Baby Boomers Survive Online Dating* and *We Gave Them Life, Now They're Trying To Take Ours: How To Talk To Adult Children Before It's Too Late*. *Sex, Meds, Livin' The Covid Life*. *Sex, Meds, Reincarnation, Livin' The Covid Life*.

Visit Eric Robespierre
at: ericrobespierre.com

www.ingramcontent.com/pod-product-compliance
Lightning Source LLC
Chambersburg PA
CBHW070933250626

47159CB00009B/3234